Copyright © 2025 Brianna Skylark

All rights reserved.

ISBN-13: 9798285242345

This is a work of fiction. Names, characters, places, and incidents either are the product of the author's imagination or are used fictitiously. Any resemblance to actual persons, living or dead, events, or locales is entirely coincidental.

Copyright © 2025 by Brianna Skylark.

All rights reserved. No part of this publication may be reproduced, distributed, or transmitted in any form or by any means, including photocopying, recording, or other electronic or mechanical methods, including information storage and retrieval systems, without the prior written permission of the author, except in the case of brief quotations embodied in critical reviews and certain other noncommercial uses permitted by copyright law.

First edition May 2025.

www.briannaskylark.com

THREE PASSENGERS FOR QUINN

An Airborne Reverse Harem Ménage

BRIANNA SKYLARK

*

Three Passengers for Quinn: An Airborne Reverse Harem Ménage is the fifth book in the **Reverse Harem Romance** series and can be read as a stand-alone novel.

Subscribe to my newsletter for a **FREE COPY** of **Play Swing**.

As the only flight attendant on a luxurious private jet, Quinn is used to catering to the rich and powerful. **But when three devastatingly handsome men board her overnight flight to Dubai,** their dark stares and wicked smiles make one thing clear - she's in for more than just a routine trip.

Carter. Laurent. Hale. **They've never shared a woman before, but Quinn is too irresistible to ignore.** At 40,000 feet, with nowhere to hide and temptation pressing in from all sides, **they make her an offer dripping with sin** - one that promises turbulence of the most **decadent** kind.

No rules. No regrets. No turning back.

CHAPTER ONE

Rain lashes against the asphalt, sending up a misty spray beneath the floodlights that line the private terminal. The air is thick with it, cold and damp, the light wind carrying the scent of jet fuel and wet pavement. The faint, distant rumble of departing aircraft echoes across the tarmac, swallowed by the steady drumming of rain against the steel skeletons of parked jets.

I clutch my umbrella tighter, tilting it just enough to shield my face from the worst of it, the wind gently catching the edge, tugging insistently as I navigate the slick ground in heels that weren't made for running. The rain is relentless, an icy kiss against the exposed skin of my legs, my pencil skirt clinging with every gust, my white blouse - neatly tucked in at the waist - feels cool against my skin, the damp air creeping beneath the crisp fabric.

Ahead, the jet looms, sleek and predatory in the downpour, its polished body reflecting the floodlights in streaks of gold and silver. The engines sit idle, their deep mechanical hum a steady undercurrent beneath the storm. The stairs glisten with water, droplets beading along the railings, pooling on each step.

I move quickly, my heels clicking sharply against the wet ground, careful but confident, ignoring the sting of the wind against my cheeks. This isn't my first storm, nor my first late-night flight, but something about the way the night feels - thick with quiet anticipation - makes the hairs at the nape of my neck stand on end.

Reaching the stairs, I pause for a breath, shifting my bag higher onto my shoulder before tucking my umbrella beneath my arm. The jet's door is open, warm air spilling out in a subtle invitation.

I ascend.

Each step takes me higher, away from the cold, from the rain, from the vast emptiness of the tarmac below, and finally, I step inside.

The warmth wraps around me instantly, a stark contrast to the bitter chill outside. The hush of the cabin swallows the storm, the heavy door somehow sealing it away like a distant memory.

Soft, dim lighting casts a golden glow over the space, accentuating the rich leather of the seats, the polished wood paneling, the curved edges of a modern, high-end interior. The jet is a masterpiece of luxury - sleek, streamlined, meticulously designed for comfort. There's no garish opulence here, no overindulgent displays of wealth. Everything is understated, but exquisite.

I breathe it in, letting the familiar scent of leather, clean linen, and faint traces of expensive cologne settle over me.

It's empty, for now.

The cockpit door is slightly ajar, a sliver of warm light spilling out, casting a narrow stripe across the aisle. Inside, the pilot and co-pilot murmur quietly, running through pre-flight checks, their voices a steady, rhythmic presence in the otherwise silent cabin.

I take a slow step forward, my heels muffled now against the plush carpeting. My fingers brush the cool leather of one of the first-class seats, a simple gesture, grounding myself in the quiet before the flight begins.

The rain hasn't let up. If anything, it's coming down harder, hammering against the fuselage in a relentless, drumming rhythm. The wind catches the tail end of the storm, sending icy gusts whipping through the open cabin door. I feel the cold creep beneath the hem of my skirt, seeping through the fine fabric of my blouse, but the warmth inside the jet is already wrapping around me, stealing the chill from my skin.

Sophie should be here by now.

I step further into the cabin, my heels clicking against the carpet, and scan the space, as if she might magically appear from thin air, but the plane is otherwise empty - eerily so. The pilots may be behind the cracked cockpit door, their voices a quiet hum of routine pre-flight chatter, but out here, it's just me.

I set my bag down in the galley and glance at my phone. No message. No missed call.

Maybe she's running late. Maybe she got held up at security, or - God forbid - the company pulled her for a different flight without telling me. They do that sometimes. But she would've let me know, wouldn't she?

I chew my lip, trying not to let the anxiety settle in my chest. She's probably fine. She'll be here any minute. And in the meantime, there's work to do.

I start with the safety checks, moving on autopilot, the steps as familiar as breathing. Fire extinguishers secured. Oxygen masks in place. First aid kit sealed and stocked. I move methodically, hands steady, even as my mind keeps drifting back to Sophie, because if she doesn't show, I'll be flying solo.

The thought makes my stomach clench. I've done single-attendant flights before, but not like this. Not with no warning, no prep. And certainly not with a roster this vague - three names and nothing else. No preferences, no notes, no hints at what kind of passengers I'm about to greet.

Carter. Laurent. Hale.

I frown as I straighten a seatbelt across the plush leather of one of the first-class chairs. It's unusual. Normally, we get at least a short dossier. Some of these high-profile clients have entire files full of instructions - how they like their drinks poured, whether they want their meal plated or straight from the packaging, how much eye contact is too much.

But this time? Nothing.

I take a breath and keep moving. The bar is next, bottles perfectly arranged, labels forward. I run a finger along the polished wood, half-expecting to find a smudge or imperfection. Of course, there isn't one. The cleaners would have taken care of that. But Sophie and I always do one last pass, a habit we developed after too many rushed turnovers.

It should be both of us here now, checking every detail, making sure everything is perfect. I should hear her beside me, muttering about how the clients better be hot if they're going to be this mysterious.

Instead, it's just me.

I press my lips together and turn back to the galley. At least the catering is fully stocked. The champagne is already chilling, the in-flight meals plated with their usual level of absurd precision. Tonight's menu is what you'd expect on a flight like this - caviar, filet mignon, something delicate and gold-dusted for dessert. Luxury, wrapped in silence.

I glance at my phone again.

Still nothing.

My fingers tighten around the edge of the counter as unease coils low in my stomach.

'Come on, Sophie. Where are you?'

I step back, exhaling, and smooth down my uniform. It's fine. If she's not here in five minutes, I'll call her.

But even as I move toward the cockpit, checking the last of the settings in the cabin - seat adjustments, lighting, temperature - I can't shake the feeling that I'm waiting for more than just my co-worker.

I'm waiting for the moment the silence shatters.

Because soon, the passengers will be here.

And something tells me this flight will be different.

I push open the door.

The cockpit is warm, a sliver of golden light spilling into the dim cabin, and as I step inside, the scent of coffee and worn leather greets me.

Captain Reynolds doesn't turn right away, his focus on the flight plan, but Callum - his co-pilot - glances over his shoulder and smirks.

'There she is,' he says.

I roll my eyes but can't stop the small smile that tugs at my lips. 'Should've known you were on this rotation.'

'And here I was, thinking you'd be happy to see me,' Callum says, shifting in his seat to face me fully. His hazel eyes gleam with the kind of easy confidence that makes everything feel just a little more relaxed.

'Depends. Are you going to be tolerable tonight?'

'Probably not,' he admits, grinning. 'But I can promise I'll be charming about it.'

I let out a soft laugh and shake my head. It's always like this with Callum - light, easy banter that makes the long flights pass quicker. We've worked together plenty of times, enough that I know he flirts just to amuse himself, never with any real expectation behind it.

Reynolds finally turns in his seat, his gaze steady and unreadable. 'You all set in the cabin?'

'Mostly. Still waiting on Sophie to show up.'

Callum frowns slightly. 'Sophie?'

'Yeah, she was supposed to be working this flight with me, but she's not answering her phone,' I lean against the frame of the door, crossing my arms. 'Tell me you've seen her.'

Reynolds shakes his head. 'She's not on the roster. You're solo tonight.'

I blink. 'What? Since when?'

'Since as long as I've had the flight plan,' he turns back to his controls. 'Someone must have switched her out.'

My stomach tightens. Flight crew swaps happen sometimes, but Sophie always gives me a heads-up if she gets reassigned. Even if she was pulled last minute, she'd have sent a text. I glance at my phone again.

Still nothing.

'You alright?' Callum asks, studying me.

I push the worry down. 'Yeah. Just wish someone had told me.'

'Guess that means you'll have to rely on us if you need anything,' he says with a lopsided smile. 'And I do make an excellent cup of coffee.'

'Now that I'll believe when I see it.'

Callum presses a hand to his chest, mock-offended. 'I'm hurt. Deeply.'

Reynolds makes a sound suspiciously like a suppressed laugh before focusing back on his instruments.

'Anyway,' I say, shaking off the nerves still prickling under my skin. 'What do we know about our passengers?'

Callum and Reynolds exchange a glance - just a flicker of something unspoken. Not enough to set off alarm bells, but enough to make me take notice.

'You don't know?' Reynolds asks, lifting a brow.

'I got names, that's about it. No dossier. No special requests.'

Reynolds exhales, shaking his head slightly. 'Figures.'

I frown. 'Why? Who are they?'

'Carter, Laurent, Hale,' Reynolds recites. 'Carter's some tech guy - built some kind of predictive algorithm for market investments. Smart enough that people throw money at him just to stay ahead of the curve.'

The name is vaguely familiar. I've heard it before, though I don't follow the finance world closely enough to know the details.

'Laurent's an art dealer - friend of his. Big money. Not the kind of guy who bids at auctions - the kind who makes deals in back rooms, where no one asks questions.'

A flicker of recognition. His name has come up in whispers before, associated with high-profile private sales, sometimes even stolen pieces. But that's all just speculation.

'And Hale?'

Reynolds' fingers tap idly against the console. 'Security. Ex-military. Not the kind you hire for corporate protection - the kind you call when you want problems handled quietly.'

My stomach gives a slow, uneasy flip.

Billionaire investor. Art dealer with a questionable reputation. A man who deals in security so high-level it doesn't get mentioned in polite circles.

'And they're traveling together?' I ask.

Callum shrugs. 'Seems like it.'

'I take it they're not the type to sit quietly and sip champagne all night,' I mutter.

Reynolds smirks. 'Depends on what kind of night they're in the mood for.'

I raise a brow. 'You've flown them before?'

'Once.'

'And?'

He doesn't answer right away, which tells me everything.

A gust of wind rattles the rain against the windshield, and I glance out at the tarmac just as headlights appear through the downpour. A sleek, black car pulls up to the base of the stairs, its surface gleaming wet beneath the floodlights. The doors don't open right away.

I inhale slowly, smoothing my hands down the front of my uniform. The last few minutes of quiet press down around me, stretching thin.

'Well,' Callum murmurs. 'Looks like you're about to find out for yourself.'

The stationary headlights cut through the rain, bouncing off the slick tarmac in long streaks of silver. From the cockpit, I have a clear view of the car, its engine humming low beneath the steady rhythm of the downpour.

I shouldn't be watching.

But I am.

I stay just inside the cockpit door, peering through the side window, my fingers curling lightly against the frame. The angle is perfect - high enough to see down onto the runway without being obvious, the soft glow from inside the jet keeping me mostly in shadow.

Outside, the driver steps into the storm, shoulders hunched against the rain as he quickly opens a large black umbrella. He moves with precision, unfazed by the weather, circling the car to the rear passenger door.

The moment stretches.

There's always something about these flights, these late-night departures from the world's wealthiest, most powerful men. It's a different kind of anticipation, quieter than a commercial flight but more charged. Like something's about to begin, something that doesn't exist on any itinerary.

Then a different door swings open, and another man steps

out.

Even from above, I feel the shift in the air, the silent weight of presence.

He moves unhurriedly, unfolding himself from the car with the kind of practiced ease that comes from knowing the world will wait for him. He straightens, rain glossing the shoulders of his dark overcoat, the tailored line of his suit visible beneath it. His hair is thick and dark, neatly combed, though a few strands are already damp from the storm.

I can't see his face fully from this angle - only the way he surveys the runway, taking in the jet, the flashing lights along the perimeter, the storm rolling in heavy around us.

And then his head tilts, just slightly.

I go still.

Even from this distance, I can tell the moment his gaze finds mine. The moment he sees me watching.

My pulse trips over itself.

I know I should move. I should step back, pretend I was adjusting something, make it seem like I wasn't curious. But I don't.

I just... look back.

His expression doesn't change. He doesn't startle, doesn't react in the way most passengers might upon realising they were being observed. Instead, he just holds my gaze, steady and unreadable, as if he's studying me in return.

A cold breeze sneaks through the cracked cockpit door, but my skin is warm, heat rising at the base of my neck. Then, as smoothly as he arrived, he looks away.

Not dismissively. Not as if I wasn't worth noticing. Just as if he'd gotten what he needed from that moment.

The driver murmurs something, shifting the umbrella to shield him as they move toward the stairs.

'Careful,' Callum drawls. I blink, startled, and turn to find him watching me, his grin slow and amused. 'Showtime,' he murmurs.

I swallow, smoothing my scarf instinctively, trying to pretend like I wasn't just entranced by a man I haven't even met yet.

Get it together, Quinn.

I roll my shoulders back, inhale slowly, and turn on my heel, heading for the cabin door with a steady, practiced stride.

By the time I reach it, my professional mask is back in place.

I know instantly that he's different. The others will arrive under the shield of an umbrella, will take their time, unbothered by the storm. But this one moves with purpose, unfazed by the downpour slicking through his dark hair, drenching his shirt in rivulets.

No hesitation.

He jogs up the stairs two at a time, reaching the cabin door within seconds, moving like a man who doesn't wait for permission to enter any space.

I step back instinctively, straightening as he crosses the threshold. The storm rages behind him, but inside the cabin, the air is warm, silent.

And then his gaze finds mine.

I don't blink. I don't shift.

I know what this is - an assessment. A measured, quiet, deliberate cataloging of details. I can almost feel the weight of it, the way his eyes take in everything at once. Not just me, but the space, the exits, the positions of the pilots. But he doesn't move on as quickly as I expect.

His gaze lingers, just slightly, the deep furrow of his brow easing as if he's just registered something unexpected.

I don't let my expression change, but I hold his stare, let the moment stretch just long enough for him to know I've noticed him too.

'Mr. Hale,' I say smoothly, keeping my voice quiet, like I might spook him if I speak too loud.

He nods once, a single dip of his chin, water still dripping from his collar.

'Miss Quinn.'

His voice is deep, steady, the kind of voice that doesn't waver even in the middle of a storm.

Then, without another word, he steps past me, moving toward the cabin, the tension in the air shifting with him. He reaches the aisle, pauses, then glances back toward the open door.

Lifts a hand.

Signals the others forward.

Only then does the driver tilt his umbrella, his stance deferential as he pulls the door open.

The two men inside don't move immediately.

Not because they're hesitant - but because they can.

And when the first man does step out, it's with the kind of unhurried grace that makes it clear he's never had to rush for anything in his life.

Mr Carter moves like he owns the jet, like the entire sky belongs to him. The rain doesn't touch him, the driver's umbrella perfectly positioned to shield him from the elements. He steps forward, straightens his cuffs, casts a single sweeping glance at the plane before making his way up the stairs.

I don't let my stance change, don't shift or fidget. Instead, I offer the same warm, professional smile as he steps into the cabin, shaking off the last of the cold.

'Welcome aboard, Mr. Carter.'

His gaze flicks to mine.

It doesn't rush past me like I expected. It stays.

A slow, careful drag from my face to the scarf at my throat, then lower, tracing the neatly pressed lines of my uniform.

There's nothing overt about it, nothing inappropriate, but I feel it - like the slightest touch of heat against bare skin.

'Thank you,' he says smoothly, his voice a low current of sound beneath the hum of the aircraft. Then, without another word, he moves past me.

The last man arrives next, just as I turn back toward the door.

Mr Laurent doesn't ascend the stairs like Carter did. He takes his time, his hand sliding into his pocket, his mouth tilted at the edge, as if the rain is only a mild inconvenience and not a reason to move any faster.

Even from here, I can tell he's enjoying this - the arrival, the setting, the moment itself.

When he steps onto the jet, his gaze lands on mine, and there's something different in the way he looks at me. Not like Carter, whose attention was slow and measured. Not like Hale, whose gaze was assessing.

Laurent is interested.

Not in a way that makes me uncomfortable. Just in a way that makes it clear that he's already taking in every detail.

I smile, keeping my tone even, polished. 'Mr. Laurent. Welcome aboard.'

He exhales a quiet laugh through his nose, the smallest curve of amusement touching his lips.

'You're good at that,' he murmurs.

'At what?'

His gaze flickers with something knowing. 'Making a man feel special.'

I hold his stare just long enough to let him know he's not the first.

'It's my job to make all my passengers feel special,' I say smoothly, a hint of something playful beneath the professionalism.

He grins, slow and easy, like he's just enjoyed a private

little joke. 'And yet, I still feel like I should be flattered.'

I don't reply. I don't need to.

Because in that moment, he knows exactly how much of this game I'm willing to play.

And he likes it.

With that, he steps past me, his scent lingering - a subtle mix of something expensive and just a little dangerous.

I exhale, smoothing my hands over my uniform as I take hold of the door, pulling it round and into place. It seals with a quiet hiss, locking out the storm.

When I turn back toward the cabin, the three men are settling into their seats, peeling off coats, undoing cuffs, rolling up sleeves in that slow, comfortable way of men who are used to claiming their space.

And all three of them, in their own way, are still aware of me.

I can feel it.

I let the moment settle, let my own pulse steady, then I step forward, the warm glow of the cabin lights softening the edges of everything.

'Gentlemen,' I say, my voice smooth, inviting. 'Can I get you anything before takeoff?'

*

The jet is sealed now, the cabin door locked, the storm shut out behind us. The sound of the rain fades, replaced by the low murmur of movement - the shifting of bodies settling into seats, the rustle of coats being shed, the quiet click of cufflinks being adjusted.

I move with purpose, fluid and efficient, slipping into my role as seamlessly as I always do.

Carter has already taken the first seat, the one closest to the bar, stretching out as he flicks open the sleek leather folder in front of him. Even as he scans the documents inside, his movements are controlled, practiced - like a man who never wastes motion.

Laurent, by contrast, lounges into his seat, one arm draped over the back as he lets out a long exhale, as if the very act of traveling is something to be enjoyed rather than endured. He's already rolled his sleeves up to his forearms, his watch catching the soft cabin light.

Hale, predictably, takes the seat with the clearest view of the entire space, his back to nothing, his gaze flicking once toward the closed cockpit door before finally settling. He doesn't bother to shake the rain from his shirt - he simply absorbs the discomfort, like he's used to it.

I take a step forward, slipping effortlessly into the moment.

'Would any of you like a drink before takeoff?' I ask, my voice warm, inviting but never forced.

Carter doesn't look up right away. He's still focused on whatever's in front of him, his fingers resting lightly against his temple.

Then, smoothly, he closes the folder. 'A whiskey,' he says.

'Neat?'

His gaze flicks to mine, lingering just long enough before he nods. 'Neat.'

I turn toward the bar, but Laurent speaks before I can take another step.

'Champagne,' he says, stretching his legs out lazily. 'Something chilled.'

'Something chilled,' I repeat, just the faintest touch of playfulness in my tone. 'Of course.'

I catch the smallest smirk at the corner of his mouth before I turn, making my way to the bar.

It takes only seconds to pour - the whiskey in a perfect, measured pour over crystal, the champagne bottle uncorked with a quiet, controlled pop. I place Carter's drink first, setting it on the tray table beside him with a gentle precision.

'Macallan,' I murmur. 'Aged eighteen years. Smooth, with just a little bite.'

He lifts the glass, rolls the amber liquid with a slow tilt of his wrist. His eyes meet mine again, and there's something in his expression that I can't quite place.

'Perfect,' he says simply.

Laurent's champagne comes next, the glass placed within easy reach. He watches me as I set it down, fingers tapping lightly against his knee.

'I should've guessed you'd have good taste,' he muses.

'You'd be surprised how often I hear that.'

His smile curves, slow and appreciative. 'Would I?'

I don't answer. I don't need to.

Instead, I shift my attention toward Hale.

He hasn't requested anything, but he's watching, studying the way I interact with the others, the way I navigate the space. His posture is relaxed, but his awareness is absolute.

'Nothing for you, Mr. Hale?' I ask smoothly.

For a moment, he says nothing.

Then, finally, 'Water. Room temperature.'

Simple. Precise.

I retrieve a bottle from the galley, pouring it into a crystal glass before setting it down in front of him. He takes it without hesitation, fingers curling around the glass, and nods once.

'Thank you.'

His voice is steady, unshaken. Not impolite, but not overly familiar either.

I sense that's how he prefers things.

I step back, letting the silence settle around us for a moment.

The men fall into their own rhythm - Carter flipping back to his documents, Laurent taking a slow sip of champagne,

Hale watching.

Always watching.

The cockpit door clicks shut.

The engines hum low beneath the floor, the deep vibration filling the cabin as the aircraft systems come to life.

Takeoff is close now.

I straighten, smoothing the hem of my skirt, and let a slow, easy smile touch my lips.

'Let me know if there's anything else I can do for you, gentlemen,' I say, voice light, polished. 'We'll be in the air shortly.'

The engines hum steadily beneath me, warming, gathering power, but we're still grounded. The cabin remains motionless, cocooned in dim light and quiet luxury, the storm outside now nothing more than a muffled presence beyond the walls of the jet.

And I - probably for the first time in my career - need a moment.

I slip into the rear of the plane, my private sanctuary, and brace my hands against the cool marble of the galley counter. I inhale deeply, slow and measured, trying to settle the low thrum of heat twisting in my stomach.

I've flown hundreds of private flights. I've served celebrities, royalty, billionaires with more power in their hands than some countries. I know how to handle privilege, wealth, and even the occasional flirtation.

But this?

This is different.

It's them.

All three of them.

They're stirring something inside of me.

Carter.

A man who moves with absolute certainty, as if every room - every space - already belongs to him before he even enters it. He'd barely spared me a glance when he first boarded, and yet that single look had stayed. His gaze had been slow, deliberate, like he was measuring something unspoken. And when I spoke to him, when I set his drink down, I could feel the weight of his awareness.

He may have returned his attention to his documents, but I wasn't foolish enough to think he had stopped noticing me.

I swallow, shifting my weight, rolling the cool bottle of water between my palms.

Then there's Laurent.

Effortless, easy, indulgent.

Where Carter commands, Laurent plays. He enjoys himself, enjoys his surroundings. Enjoys me. He hadn't hidden the way he watched me, the way his lips curved just slightly every time I spoke.

Making a man feel special, he had murmured.

And I had.

Not just him.

All of them.

My pulse beats low and steady beneath my skin.

And then there's Hale.

I exhale slowly, pressing my fingertips against the cool counter, grounding myself.

Carter was deliberate. Laurent was amused.

But Hale?

He had lingered.

Not in an obvious way. Not in a way that would have made anyone else take notice. But I felt it. Felt the way his sharp, assessing gaze moved over me, not indulgent like Laurent's, not calculating like Carter's - but something else. Something heavier.

Something that told me he doesn't just watch people. He reads them.

My stomach tightens.

I shake my head. Get it together, Quinn.

I am a professional.

I know how to adjust, how to shift my energy to match the tone of a flight, to anticipate needs before they arise. I know how to make every passenger feel taken care of while keeping just enough distance to ensure nothing lingers past landing.

And that's what I'll do now.

That's what I have to do.

I inhale deeply, let my spine straighten, smooth a hand over my scarf, and step out of the galley, back into the warmth of the cabin.

The moment I do, the intercom crackles to life.

'Good evening, gentlemen,' Captain Reynolds' voice carries through the quiet space, deep and steady. 'This is your captain speaking. I'll be flying you to Dubai tonight alongside my co-pilot, Callum Hayes. We're expecting a flight time of approximately twelve hours and forty-five minutes, with a smooth route for most of the way - though we may experience some mild turbulence as we pass over the Atlantic. Nothing to be concerned about.'

I make my way down the aisle as he speaks, pausing near the bar, hands clasped gently in front of me, my polished smile back in place.

'We've received final clearance from air traffic control and will be taxiing shortly,' Reynolds continues. 'If you need anything during the flight, our attendant, Miss Quinn, will be happy to assist you.'

I nod slightly at the mention of my name, the automatic reflex of someone who has heard their introduction over the speakers a hundred times. But this time, it feels different. Because as soon as my name is spoken, I feel it again.

Carter doesn't react outwardly, but I see the small shift in his posture, the slow roll of his glass between his fingers.

Laurent tips his champagne flute slightly in my direction,

his eyes holding mine just a little too long, amusement glinting at the edges.

And Hale - still, quiet, unreadable - keeps watching.

The jet begins to move.

I steel myself.

Twelve hours and forty-five minutes.

The jet glides forward, rolling smoothly onto the taxiway, the hum of the engines deepening as we prepare for departure. Through the windows, the storm still rages, streaks of rain slashing sideways under the glow of the floodlights. Beyond them, the night stretches out in endless darkness, the city lights scattered like embers in the distance.

I stand near the bar, hands clasped loosely in front of me, my posture relaxed but my focus sharp. The men are settled now, each in their own way - Carter, still half-absorbed in his documents, Laurent, lazily twirling the stem of his champagne flute between his fingers, and Hale, ever-watchful, ever-quiet.

The intercom crackles again.

'Cabin crew, prepare for takeoff.'

Just me. I'm the crew tonight.

I move smoothly through the aisle, making final checks, ensuring everything is secure. The men barely acknowledge me as I work, but their awareness lingers - the kind that doesn't need to be obvious to be felt.

I take a seat, steap myself in. Then, the engines roar.

The force of acceleration presses lightly against me as the jet surges forward, gathering speed, streaking down the runway with a smooth, commanding power. The wheels leave the ground, and for a moment, there's weightlessness - just a fraction of a second where the world holds its breath.

Then we climb.

The jet soars, slicing through the rain-heavy air, angling steeply into the sky.

Outside, the city lights shrink, swallowed by the dark.

A pocket of turbulence rattles the plane as we break through the thick belly of the storm, the winds grasping at the fuselage, shaking us gently before releasing us into clearer air.

Laurent exhales, amused. 'Bit of a rough climb.'

I offer a calm, practiced smile. 'Nothing out of the ordinary.'

'Still,' he muses, swirling the last of his champagne, 'I think I'll need another drink to recover.'

I arch a brow. 'I'd hate for you to suffer.'

His grin widens, but before he can respond, the jet breaks free of the clouds, and suddenly - everything changes.

The storm is gone.

Replaced by a vast, glittering expanse.

Stars.

Thousands of them, stretching out in every direction, the deep indigo of the sky endless and undisturbed. The glow of the city is far below now, nothing but a faint, golden haze on the horizon. Up here, there's only silence and space, the cabin filled with the soft ambient light of the aircraft, the hum of the engines smooth and steady beneath our feet.

I glance toward the nearest window, just for a second, just to take it in.

It's always been my favorite part of flying - this moment right here. When the world disappears below, when there's nothing but sky, when it feels like you've left everything behind.

Carter shifts in his seat, rolling his shoulders slightly.

Laurent leans back, exhaling slowly.

Hale watches.

Then the intercom clicks one final time.

'We've reached cruising altitude,' Reynolds announces. 'You're free to move about the cabin.'

Three Passengers for Quinn

The seatbelt signs blink off.
And the night stretches out ahead of us, endless, waiting.

CHAPTER TWO

An hour later and the golden light of dawn filters through the cabin, spilling in through the wide windows, casting soft, shifting reflections against the polished surfaces. Below, the ocean stretches endlessly, its surface catching the first warm rays of the sun, sparkling like scattered diamonds. The hush of the aircraft is deeper now - no longer the stillness of takeoff, but something else entirely.

Something settled.

Something intimate.

I move with grace, carrying a tray of finely plated breakfast dishes from the galley, my movements fluid as I step back into the main cabin. The air inside is warm, laced with the faintest traces of fresh coffee, buttered croissants, the subtle spice of citrus zest curling from freshly squeezed juice.

The men have shifted in their seats, their postures looser, their presence still undeniably felt.

Carter is exactly where I left him, composed and self-possessed, a fresh glass of water sitting untouched beside his whiskey tumbler from earlier. Weston Hale remains quiet, his gaze drifting to the horizon beyond the windows, his hands wrapped loosely around a cup of black coffee.

But Laurent-

Laurent is the only one who looks like he's been waiting for me.

He lounges back into his seat, one arm draped carelessly along the headrest, his shirt now unbuttoned at the collar, the cuffs of his sleeves rolled up his forearms. There's a sleekness to him, a slow, unhurried ease, like a man who has never been forced to rush for anything in his life.

And he's watching me.

Not overtly. Not in a way that crosses any lines. But in a way that feels just a little too pointed.

'Your breakfast, Mr. Laurent,' I say smoothly, setting his plate down in front of him.

His lips twitch, but he doesn't press whatever is on his mind. Instead, he glances down at his meal - perfectly poached eggs, golden and trembling, slices of fresh baguette, a delicate array of seasonal fruits carefully arranged on the side.

'Beautiful,' he murmurs. I'm about to respond when his gaze flicks back to me. 'Tell me, Quinn...' he says, the syllables of my name rolling smoothly from his tongue. 'Do you ever get to enjoy this?'

I blink, caught off guard. 'Enjoy what?'

He gestures vaguely. 'This. The luxury. The endless string of flights to the world's most expensive places. You must see so much, but do you ever *experience* it?'

His tone is light, casual, but I feel the weight beneath it - the way he's testing, the way he's pulling.

'My job is to ensure you enjoy it,' I reply smoothly, adjusting a small silver coffee spoon beside his plate.

He hums lightly, considering me. 'And do you?'

I tilt my head slightly. 'Do I what?'

'Enjoy serving?'

The way he says it - soft, thoughtful, but with the barest edge of something else - makes my stomach tighten.

I know exactly what he's doing.

I've seen it before, this kind of slow, lazy play. It's a different kind of power than Carter's cold precision or Hale's quiet command.

Laurent doesn't conquer. He lures.

And worse - he makes you want it.

I exhale, offering the smallest smile, just enough to keep the balance. 'I take pride in my work, Mr. Laurent.'

'Pride isn't the same as pleasure though, is it?'

I meet his gaze head-on, holding it steady, unshaken.

'They're not so different,' I say lightly, setting his drink down beside his plate.

His fingers shift, just barely - and in that fraction of a second, his touch brushes against mine.

A barely-there stroke of warm skin against skin.

The moment is small. Fleeting. But it lands. And he knows it.

I inhale through my nose, slow and controlled, ignoring the way my pulse has decided to misbehave. I step back, as poised as ever-

But just as I move, his hand grazes lightly against the silk of my skirt.

Not deliberate.

Not forceful.

Just a featherlight touch, an accident that isn't entirely accidental.

I don't react.

I refuse to react.

Instead, I simply shift, stepping away without hesitation,

without lingering.

But I feel the weight of his attention still on me, even as I move toward the next seat.

And when I glance back - just once - his lips are curled at the edges, his head tilted slightly, watching me like he's only just getting started.

The scent of warm espresso and crisp, buttered bread lingers in the air as I step away from Laurent, smoothing my hands over my uniform, steadying myself.

One down.

I move toward the next seat, toward Hale.

He hasn't spoken much, hasn't indulged in the easy banter the way Laurent has. Even now, he sits slightly apart from the others, his posture relaxed but alert, his attention turned toward the window.

For a moment, I hesitate, my tray still balanced perfectly in my hands, my steps slowing. Because Hale isn't just looking outside. He's absorbing it.

The golden glow of dawn spills over the curve of the horizon, washing the sky in soft gradients of peach and pink, glinting off the distant ocean below like molten gold. It's a sight I've seen hundreds of times before - a privilege of working these flights - but watching him take it in is something else entirely.

His expression isn't unreadable now.

It's softened.

Not unguarded, not exposed, but... something close.

As if, for a moment, he's forgotten the rest of the world exists.

And then, in the quiet hush of the cabin, the sunlight shifts - and his gaze slides from the horizon to me.

My breath catches before I can stop it.

Because whatever appreciation had been in his stare for the dawn outside - whatever quiet awe he had for the way the sky bloomed with light - it's turned on me now.

Not sharp. Not overt.

Just full.

Full in a way that makes something deep inside me tighten, heat curling low in my stomach before I can push it away.

I school my features quickly, offering my usual composed smile as I step forward and set his breakfast in front of him. Perfectly scrambled eggs, smoked salmon on lightly toasted rye, a side of avocado drizzled with citrus.

Clean.

Balanced.

Just like him.

'Your breakfast, Mr. Hale,' I say, keeping my tone smooth.

He doesn't look at the plate.

He's still looking at me.

A slow blink, a small shift in his expression, and then-

'Do you like flying?'

The question is so unexpected that it catches me completely off guard.

My pulse jumps.

'Pardon?' I murmur, straightening, unsure if I heard him correctly.

Hale leans back slightly in his seat, finally breaking eye contact as he reaches for his coffee, his fingers wrapping around the ceramic with easy control.

'Flying,' he repeats, tilting his head toward the window. 'Do you like it?'

I stare for a second, unsure why this question feels different than all the others. It's harmless. Simple.

And yet, I feel like there's something else beneath it.

I exhale softly, shifting my weight, adjusting my posture as if that will stop my heart from racing.

'I love it,' I answer honestly. 'There's something... freeing about it. Watching the world from above, slipping between places like the space between doesn't exist. It's peaceful.'

Hale hums quietly, swirling the coffee in his mug. He doesn't respond right away, and I don't know why that makes me more nervous than if he'd disagreed with me.

Then-

'It's lonely too, though.'

The words slip out, quiet, thoughtful.

And that is what makes my stomach tighten.

Not the statement itself, but the way he says it.

Like he knows.

Like he's felt it.

And the way his eyes find mine again - low, steady, deep - like he can see right through me.

I shift, straighten. 'I suppose that depends on who you're flying with.'

Hale watches me for another long second before finally - finally - breaking the moment himself.

He lifts his coffee, takes a slow sip, and nods once.

'Fair enough,' he murmurs.

And just like that, I can breathe again.

But as I step away, moving toward Carter's seat, my heart is still beating far too fast.

Two down.

One to go.

Carter.

He hasn't moved much since takeoff, his body still composed, controlled, the very picture of quiet authority. His empty whiskey tumbler has been replaced with a glass of water, the condensation beading along its surface, untouched. A tablet sits on the armrest beside him, the screen dark now, as though he's abandoned whatever business had once held his focus.

And yet, he isn't distracted.

Not the way Laurent is, sinking lazily into his seat, letting his amusement play out through teasing remarks. Not the way Hale had been, absorbed in the sky outside, caught in something deep and distant.

Carter is present.

And watching.

His gaze finds mine before I even reach him.

It's measured, the way he looks at me. Like he's weighing something unseen, turning it over in his mind. Like he's looking for cracks in a façade he already knows I'm wearing. And yet, despite the intensity of his stare, it isn't unkind.

It's curious.

And somehow, that's worse.

'Your breakfast, Mr. Carter,' I say smoothly, setting his plate down.

His meal is precisely arranged, every element executed with quiet perfection. Poached eggs, still perfectly domed, sit atop a crisp English muffin, draped in the faintest sheen of hollandaise. Beside them, slices of honey-glazed ham, neatly layered. Nothing excessive. Nothing indulgent. Efficient. Balanced.

Just like him.

I step back, expecting him to glance at his food the way Hale had - assessing but uninterested in the details. But he doesn't look down.

He looks at me.

And doesn't stop.

'How long have you been flying, Quinn?'

His voice is smooth, low. A question that should be simple, but somehow isn't.

I blink once, keeping my expression neutral, my hands clasped lightly in front of me.

'Nearly six years now,' I reply. 'I started in commercial before transitioning to private.'

Carter hums, finally shifting his gaze - not away, just lower.

His eyes flick over me slowly, not in an inappropriate way, but in a way that feels thorough.

'And you enjoy it?' he asks, echoing Hale's earlier question.

I keep my voice even. 'It has its rewards.'

His lips press together slightly, almost like he's considering that response.

Then, after a pause-

'Is that why you're still doing it?'

I still, just for a fraction of a second. Because that might be the difference between Carter and the other two.

Laurent plays with his words, lures you in gently, makes you want to answer him, even if you know it's dangerous.

Hale doesn't pry, he watches, waits for you to say something you didn't mean to say.

But Carter-

Carter doesn't ask what you're willing to share. He asks what you don't expect to reveal.

I lift my chin slightly, keeping my expression smooth, unreadable. 'It's a good career.'

'A safe answer.'

My stomach tightens.

'A true one,' I say lightly, adjusting the placement of his silverware.

'Mmm.'

It's a small sound, noncommittal, as if he doesn't believe me but is willing to let it slide.

For now.

But before I can move away, before I can regain the space that suddenly feels much too small-

The plane shudders.

It's nothing major, just a brief pocket of air, but it's enough to make me shift, my balance instinctively adjusting-

And then there's warmth.

A hand - his hand - reaching out, steadying me.

His fingers graze the inside of my wrist, lightly, barely there, but still enough to send a sharp jolt of sensation skating up my spine, down the back of my neck, curling low in my stomach.

For a moment, I can't move.

I just stand there, my pulse suddenly too loud, the cabin feeling smaller, the hush deeper.

His grip isn't forceful. Not demanding.

Just… anchoring.

A simple touch, a moment of balance, a reflexive motion-

But it lingers.

Just a fraction of a second longer than it should. Long enough that we both feel it.

Then, smoothly, he withdraws, fingers barely brushing the silk of my sleeve as he does.

'Careful,' he murmurs, his voice lower now.

I inhale sharply, stepping back. 'Nothing I can't handle.'

He holds my gaze, and for a moment, I swear I see something shift behind his eyes. Then- a slow, deliberate nod. As if I've passed some kind of test.

I clear my throat, stepping away, retreating toward the bar, my heart still pounding despite my perfectly even breaths.

Three men.

Three different energies.

And all three of them are affecting me.

And the worst part?

I think they know it.

*

The light has changed again.

It's no longer the soft gold of dawn creeping across the

horizon, no longer the fragile blush of morning stretching over the ocean below. Now, the sun is fully awake, spilling bold streams of light through the jet's wide windows, illuminating the cabin in rich amber tones. The sky outside is endless - bright, blue, stretching infinitely in every direction - and the water below sparkles like shattered glass, the reflection of daylight rippling across its surface.

Inside, the hush of earlier has shifted into something warmer, something looser.

The men have gathered together now, taking up the main seating area, a quiet, easy energy settling between them.

They aren't spread out anymore - no longer three separate presences, distinct and unspoken.

Now, they've shifted together, their postures more at ease, the air between them richer with familiarity, a shared rhythm forming in their conversation.

Laurent stretches back into his seat, one arm draped carelessly over the headrest, a lazy smirk playing at the edge of his lips. Carter sits upright, composed but relaxed, one ankle resting lightly over his knee, his fingers curled around the base of a fresh cup of coffee. And Hale - even Hale - has settled slightly, his usual stillness punctuated by quiet smirks, the occasional flicker of amusement shadowing his sharp features.

And they're laughing.

Deep, quiet chuckles from Carter. Low, teasing remarks from Laurent. Hale's lips barely tilting into something close to a smile, but a smile nonetheless.

The shift is so subtle, so natural, that I almost don't notice it at first.

But I do.

Because it means something. It means they aren't just colleagues, aren't just men who happen to be sharing this flight. They know each other.

They fit.

And I feel it now - the magnetism between them.

It's different from the kind of presence I'm used to on flights like this. Normally, a jet full of powerful men is a silent war of egos, a room filled with tense, unspoken competition, each one wanting to outmaneuver the other.

But this?

This is smoother. There's an ease between them, an unspoken understanding, a gravitational pull that keeps them moving in sync, orbiting one another. And somehow, I feel it too.

From the bar, I keep my hands busy, pretending not to listen, pretending I don't feel the pull of their voices, the way their laughter moves through me like a slow, rolling wave.

I retrieve a fresh tray, polishing the already-pristine glasses, adjusting the angle of a carafe, ensuring everything is in perfect order.

I don't need to.

But I need something to do.

Because there's a heat growing under my skin, something warm, something dangerous, and I know they feel it too.

Even if they haven't said it yet.

The light of mid-morning stretches across the cabin, catching the soft gleam of crystal glasses, the rich mahogany of the tables, the quiet shimmer of the ocean far below.

'I'm not saying it isn't revolutionary,' Carter says smoothly, his voice measured, calm. 'But progress isn't driven by idealism. It's driven by leverage. Data is leverage. Control the flow of information, and you control everything that follows.'

Laurent scoffs lightly, ever the playful adversary, his fingers spinning the base of his empty espresso cup against the tabletop.

'Technology doesn't dictate progress,' he counters, his grin widening as if he's waiting for Carter to take the bait. 'Art does. Ideas do. Creativity moves the world forward, not a bunch of algorithms and data streams.'

Hale, silent up until now, exhales slowly. 'Art is history. Technology is the future.'

Laurent raises an eyebrow, studying him. 'And where does that leave the present?'

Hale doesn't answer immediately. Instead, he takes a slow sip of his coffee, the weight of his silence stretching.

Then, finally-

'Negotiable.'

Laurent's laughter is low, easy. 'That's such a military answer.'

Hale shrugs, unbothered.

'You're both missing the point,' Carter cuts in smoothly, swirling the last of his own coffee. 'It's about power, not philosophy. People don't innovate because they want to create. They innovate because they want to own.'

Laurent shakes his head. 'How bleak. No one creates anything of value without passion.'

'They do when there's money behind it,' Carter counters, arching a brow. 'Look at the Renaissance - patronage drove the most celebrated works of art in history. Without financial backing, half the world's masterpieces wouldn't exist.'

Laurent smirks. 'You're not seriously suggesting that wealth is the foundation of art.'

Carter gives a slow, deliberate nod. 'I'm suggesting it's the gatekeeper.'

I keep working, listening, adjusting the angle of a tray that doesn't need adjusting, polishing the edge of an already-gleaming glass.

The back-and-forth between them is mesmerising - so effortless, so fluid, the rhythm so natural that I realise this isn't the first time they've had this kind of debate.

And then-

Laurent leans back in his seat, tipping his head slightly, his grin widening.

'Doesn't matter either way,' he muses, his voice smooth, lazy, knowing. 'At the end of the day, every great empire, every great invention, every great masterpiece-'

He pauses, letting the moment stretch, letting Carter and Hale both wait for it.

Then-

'-was inspired by a man trying to impress a woman.'

The statement is so absurdly confident, so casually, frustratingly arrogant, that it slips past my filter before I can stop it.

I scoff.

It's small. Barely audible.

But not small enough.

The air shifts.

I freeze.

My fingers tighten around the edge of the silver tray, my heart lodging itself high in my throat as I realise - far too late - what I've just done.

The conversation stops.

Three pairs of eyes turn to me.

And suddenly - I've stepped into the ring.

I feel it immediately - the weight of their attention, the shift in their postures, the slow, deliberate way Carter tilts his head, Laurent's amusement deepening, Hale's stillness becoming heavier.

'Something to add, Miss Quinn?'

Carter's voice is smooth, calm, calculated, but the undertone - the weight behind it - sends a quiet shiver down my spine.

I exhale slowly, already working to recover, slipping my practiced mask back into place.

'I didn't mean to interrupt,' I say lightly, keeping my voice even, professional, polished. 'Please, continue.'

But Laurent grins.

And that grin tells me - it's too late.

'Oh, but now I *have* to know,' he muses, leaning forward, elbows on his knees, his stare all but pinning me in place. 'Tell me, then. What inspires a woman?'

'I don't think that would be appropriate,' I say smoothly, already turning away, already working to slip back into my place at the periphery-

But Carter shifts.

Just slightly.

His fingers tap once against his empty cup, his expression unreadable. 'You weren't concerned about appropriateness when you scoffed.'

My stomach tightens.

Laurent's eyes gleam, sensing blood.

Hale tilts his head, his gaze steady, unreadable. 'Go on,' he murmurs. Low. Inviting. A challenge.

And just like that-

I've lost control of the moment.

They're waiting now.

Watching.

And I'm the centre of their gravity.

*

The air stretches, tightens - a moment too long, a moment I wasn't supposed to create.

Three men.

Three minds sharper than steel.

And now, I'm in their sights.

'Go on,' Hale murmurs, his voice low, steady. 'Speak freely.'

There's a hum of expectation between them now - an

energy that wasn't there before.

Carter watches me, gaze assessing, as if I'm a variable he didn't account for.

Laurent's grin lingers, slow and lazy, but his eyes are sharper now, waiting for me to bite.

Hale, ever silent, is the hardest to read. But there's something in the way he watches me - something that tells me he's listening more closely than anyone else.

I shouldn't say anything.

I should retreat, give them a polite smile, let the conversation slip away from me.

But I don't.

Because the way Laurent's words sit in the air, the way they challenge and provoke, the way they demand a reaction-

It's too much to ignore. So, before I can stop myself-

'Maybe that's the real problem,' I murmur.

Their attention sharpens instantly.

'Oh?' Laurent leans forward slightly, his amusement flickering, his curiosity deepening. 'Do tell.'

I inhale, steadying myself, choosing my words carefully.

'You assume that every major innovation, every empire, every invention exists because a man was trying to impress a woman,' I tilt my head slightly, keeping my tone even, controlled, though I feel my pulse quickening. 'But what if that's just another form of ego? A way to romanticise the idea that men only create because they want to be admired?'

Laurent's grin widens. 'And what's the alternative?'

'That sometimes,' I say, carefully setting down my tray. 'Things are built - not out of ambition, not out of desire - but out of necessity.'

Carter studies me now, his fingers idly tracing the rim of his glass. 'Explain.'

I feel my stomach tighten. This is dangerous.

But I'm already in too deep.

'Some of the most important innovations in history,' I say, choosing my words with precision, 'weren't created out of a desire to impress or to gain power. They were created because someone had to make them.'

Carter doesn't blink. 'Give me an example.'

I exhale softly, forcing my mind to focus. I've read enough, seen enough, learned enough to hold my own - at least for a moment.

'Ada Lovelace,' I say, lifting my chin slightly. 'She wrote what's considered the first algorithm. Not because she wanted to gain power, not because she was trying to impress anyone - but because she saw something no one else did. She understood the potential of technology before the world even had a framework for it.'

Laurent tilts his head, intrigued. 'That's an awfully convenient example.'

'And yet,' I counter. 'It's a true one.'

Carter's gaze sharpens. 'And what about motivation? Surely no one invents something without the drive to see it recognised.'

'Recognition and necessity aren't mutually exclusive,' I reply. 'Plenty of discoveries happen because people are trying to solve problems, not just to be remembered for solving them.'

I feel all three of them watching me now, differently than before.

Laurent's grin is slower this time, his fingers tapping lightly against his knee, his interest shifting.

Carter nods, just slightly, like I've passed some unspoken test.

Hale - Hale just watches, quiet, his eyes holding something unreadable.

I inhale, stepping back, suddenly hyper-aware of myself again, of my uniform, my role, the fact that I shouldn't be engaging this way.

Because if Sophie were here-

My breath catches in my throat, the thought slicing through me.

If Sophie were here, this wouldn't be happening. Because Sophie would have jumped in immediately. She would have turned the conversation into something playful, reckless, teasing. She would have flirted outright, laughed boldly, taken the heat off me.

She would have been brilliant.

And I-

I wouldn't be the centre of their focus right now. I wouldn't be standing here, pulse racing, throat dry, mind caught in something I don't fully understand. I wouldn't be letting this happen.

'I should check on the galley,' I say, voice smooth, detached, as if I hadn't just let them see more than I intended.

I turn, moving before any of them can stop me, my heart hammering as I slip away from their orbit. But I feel it. Even as I move back to the safety of my workspace. Even as I force myself to calm down. Even as I pretend that I didn't just do something irreversible.

But just as I force my body to step away, a voice stops me.

'Stay.'

It's Laurent.

Smooth. Easy. Like he's not asking me to cross some invisible line - like it's the most natural thing in the world.

I hesitate.

And that hesitation costs me. Because now, I feel them watching again.

Laurent - grinning, relaxed, the effortless temptation of him curling in the air between us.

Carter - silent, composed, but considering. Weighing something. Waiting to see what I'll do.

Hale - still, unreadable, but his presence anchors the space, makes it feel smaller, heavier, inevitable.

I wet my lips, my pulse slow but hard, steady but uncertain.

'I have work to do,' I say lightly, my practiced excuse, but I don't move.

Laurent tilts his head, his smirk deepening. 'It's a long flight. You can spare a moment.'

Carter leans back slightly, his expression unreadable, but his attention sharp. 'Unless there's a rule against it.'

My stomach tightens.

There isn't.

I know that.

I know the lines. The boundaries. I know what is technically allowed and what is simply never done. Sophie would know, too. And if she were here-

She would sit.

She would slide into the open seat with a dramatic sigh, toss her hair over her shoulder, and stretch out like she belonged there. She would laugh boldly, would turn the teasing right back on them, would let herself indulge in the attention. She would make it look so easy.

I could join them, just for a moment.

I could let myself have this - just this once.

Who would know?

I inhale, slow and shallow, conflicted in a way I wasn't expecting. Not just because they're beautiful men with sharp minds and piercing eyes, with voices that move like honey and silk. But because for the first time in so long...

I don't feel invisible.

I don't feel like I'm floating above the world, serving it but never part of it.

I feel seen.

And that's dangerous.

Because I can't afford to be seen.

I hesitate too long - and Laurent sees it.

His smirk flickers into something softer, something almost knowing. Then he leans forward, resting his arms on his knees, his fingers steepled together.

'You know,' he muses, his voice low, lazy, 'I think you'd enjoy it.'

I lift my chin, forcing my voice to stay steady, neutral. 'Enjoy what?'

Laurent's smile is damn near devastating.

'Being in the conversation, instead of just listening to it.'

The words land deep, striking somewhere I wasn't prepared to be struck, because he's right.

I should say no.

I should excuse myself, retreat with grace, slip back into the polished professionalism I wear so well.

But I don't.

So, instead of walking away, instead of ignoring the slow, steady heat building under my skin, I inhale - deep, steady, deliberate - and I sit. It's not bold, not theatrical. No dramatic sigh, no flirtatious stretch of limbs like Sophie would have done.

Just a quiet, controlled movement, a single choice that changes everything.

Because the moment I sink into the empty seat, the moment my body settles into the warmth of the leather, the moment I allow myself to exist in their space rather than just orbit it, I feel their attention.

Laurent grins, slow and victorious, his head tipping slightly, studying me like I've just become his favorite new discovery. Carter watches me without reaction, without a shift in posture or expression, but I see it in his eyes. A quiet flicker of something - not approval, not surprise, but intrigue.

And Hale-

Hale does nothing.

Doesn't smirk, doesn't tease, doesn't comment.

But his gaze?

It lingers.

It absorbs.

It takes.

And I feel it everywhere.

I cross my legs carefully, adjusting my posture, smoothing the hem of my skirt where it rests over my thighs. Their eyes follow the movement. I refuse to let it unnerve me.

'There,' Laurent says smoothly, tipping his glass toward me in a mock toast. 'That wasn't so hard, was it?'

I exhale softly, arching a brow. 'The way you were talking, I half expected a contract to sign.'

Laurent's laughter is low, easy. 'Tempting. But I much prefer verbal agreements.'

'Is that how you operate?' I muse, tilting my head. 'All charm and no paperwork?'

Carter makes a sound that's almost a chuckle, deep in his throat. Laurent looks delighted.

'A woman after my own heart,' he murmurs.

'Dangerous assumption,' I counter, resting my hands lightly on my lap. 'Who says I'm after anything?'

Carter sets his drink down slowly, the weight of his gaze pressing into me like a physical force. 'You came after our argument well enough.'

My pulse skips.

Because he's right.

I had stepped in, answered, challenged them, without hesitation.

Without thinking about it.

And now, I'm sitting in their space, engaging with them, matching them - exactly as they do with each other.

I swallow, holding Carter's stare. 'Only because Laurent

invited me to.'

'Don't blame him for your own curiosity,' Carter replies smoothly.

I should be unnerved by him.

By the way he wields his words like a blade - sharp, precise, cutting exactly where he means to.

But I'm not.

Because I know how to wield mine too.

I lean back slightly, tilting my chin. 'You don't like unexpected variables, do you?'

Laurent makes a delighted sound.

Hale - silent as always - watches me closer.

Carter, to his credit, doesn't react outwardly. But I see the tension in his fingers, the way his mouth moves like he's considering something deeper than what I said.

Then, after a moment-

'No,' he says simply. 'I don't.'

The honesty of it startles me.

And something about that tiny flicker of vulnerability, that admission, makes the air even warmer than before.

Laurent, sensing the shift, leans in slightly, his eyes gleaming. 'You're full of surprises, aren't you, Quinn?'

'I prefer to think of myself as adaptable,' I say lightly.

'*Mmm*,' his gaze dips lower, just barely, a slow, measured flicker down my neck, over my collarbone, the subtle press of my blouse against my frame.

The movement is so slight, so controlled, that I almost don't register it.

Almost.

Then he looks back up - and he knows.

I know that he knows.

And I hate that my stomach tightens at the realization.

The cabin feels smaller now.

The air heavier.

I let a slow breath pass through my lips, ignoring the way my skin feels warmer than before.

I shouldn't stay much longer.

I shouldn't let this pull me in further.

But before I can move, before I can think of an excuse to leave-

Hale speaks.

Quiet. Low.

And for the first time all night, it's not a statement.

It's a question.

'What else do you know?'

*

The words settle between us, a different kind of challenge. Not teasing, not playful, not a test.

Something else.

Something heavier.

And I don't know how to answer.

Because I think he's not just asking about history, or art, or technology.

I think he's asking about me.

And that is far more dangerous.

The air is too thick now, too warm - charged with something I shouldn't be indulging.

Hale's question lingers, heavier than it should be.

What else do you know?

I could ignore it. I could brush it off, slip back behind the mask of professionalism, remind them - and myself - that I do not belong in this conversation.

But I don't.

Because the truth is, I know exactly what I'm doing.

I exhale softly, letting my eyes sweep over them. One, then the other, then the last.

And I answer.

'I know that Mr Carter doesn't like surprises,' I say first, letting my gaze land on him, steady and unshaken. 'He operates with absolute control because he believes control is the only way to ensure success. Unpredictability is a weakness, and he doesn't tolerate weakness.'

Carter doesn't react. Not outwardly. But the faintest flicker of something - a sharp, dark gleam in his eyes - tells me he wasn't expecting that.

'And Mr Laurent-' I turn my attention next, watching as his lips curve slightly, his amusement deepening, '-he thrives on unpredictability. He welcomes it, invites it, tempts it closer just to see what happens next. He doesn't believe in control, because control is boring. And Mr Laurent hates to be bored.'

Laurent's smile widens, lazy and wolfish, his fingers tapping lightly against his knee. 'Go on,' he murmurs.

I inhale slowly.

And then I turn to Hale.

His stillness is sharper now, heavier. He hasn't said a word, hasn't moved, but I feel the quiet weight of his attention pressing into me like gravity.

I lift my chin slightly. 'And Mr Hale-'

A pause.

A moment too long.

Because Hale is different.

Carter and Laurent let you see what they want you to see. They shape the air around them, bend perception to their will, play their parts with flawless execution.

But Hale-

Hale is unreadable.

So I say the only thing I know for certain.

'Hale doesn't waste words. Because he doesn't need to.'

A slow, controlled blink.

The faintest tilt of his head.

And then-

'Smart girl,' he murmurs.

The words slip under my skin, slide down my spine in a way they shouldn't.

I let out a breath, smoothing my hands over my skirt, forcing myself to remain composed.

Laurent shifts suddenly, pushing to his feet in a single, fluid motion.

'Now that,' he says, moving toward the bar, 'deserves a drink.'

I watch him saunter across the cabin, rolling up his sleeves as he reaches for a bottle of something rich and amber-colored, his movements deliberate, unhurried.

I shouldn't let him.

I should tell him no, should remind them that I am not here to be entertained.

But I don't.

Because the way he looks at me now-

Like I'm something worth savouring, worth taking his time with-

It sets fire to something I don't want to name.

He pours slowly, his fingers wrapped loosely around the crystal decanter, the liquid glistening as it spills into the glass.

Then he turns, stepping back toward me, and his eyes never leave mine.

He holds the drink out, an invitation that is so much more than just an offering.

For a second, I don't move.

Then- I take it.

Laurent settles back into his seat, watching me as I lift the glass to my lips, as I let the warmth of the liquor slide across my tongue, down my throat, pooling heat in my stomach.

And they are all watching now.

Not just watching-

Devouring.

I set the glass down carefully, aware of the silence, aware of the shift, aware that I have let something irreversible happen.

Laurent leans in slightly, his voice low, almost indulgent.

The whiskey is warm in my stomach, but the heat curling low in my spine has nothing to do with the drink.

It's them.

Their attention.

The way Laurent lounges back, watching me with pure satisfaction, his fingers tapping lightly against the rim of his glass.

The way Carter leans forward just slightly, elbows resting on the table, his gaze sharp, assessing, turning something over in his mind.

The way Hale doesn't move, doesn't speak - but somehow still takes up all the space in the room.

Their focus is heavy, pressing, curling around me like a slow burn.

And the worst part?

I let it happen.

I should have walked away. I should have left the moment intact, let them have their conversation, let them keep their games between themselves.

But I didn't.

I sat.

I spoke.

I indulged.

And now I can't take it back.

Laurent smirks, dragging his finger along the rim of his glass, his voice low, smooth, indulgent.

'You spend so much time in the sky, Quinn,' he muses, his words measured and deliberate, a tease curling beneath them. 'Slipping between places, watching the world move beneath you.'

He lifts his glass, watching the whiskey shift before bringing his gaze back to mine.

'But tell me this-'

A pause. A breath.

And then-

'Have you ever let yourself fall?'

The air changes.

Not suddenly. Not violently.

Slowly. Thickly. Completely.

I inhale too sharply, too fast.

Laurent's smirk widens.

Carter watches me too closely.

And Hale-

Hale doesn't react.

But I feel it.

The weight of his attention.

I know what Laurent is asking.

And I know it has nothing to do with flying.

I should let the question hang, let it dissolve into silence, let it disappear before it can mean something more.

But I don't.

Because suddenly - recklessly - I want to play.

I lift my glass, rolling my wrist just slightly, watching the whiskey catch the light.

Then I meet his gaze, steady and unshaken.

And I say, slow and smooth-

'Not yet.'

The silence erupts into something molten.

Something sharp and deep and impossibly hot.

Laurent inhales softly, his smirk flickering at the edges, like he wasn't expecting that - but loves that he got it anyway.

Carter still doesn't move.

Doesn't react.

But his fingers tighten just slightly against his glass.

And Hale-

Hale finally speaks again.

Quiet. Low.

A question that destroys me.

'Would you like to?'

My pulse stumbles.

Like it doesn't know where to go, like it's been thrown off rhythm, like I was prepared for the heat but not for the fire.

Hale doesn't move, doesn't blink, doesn't shift. He just looks at me like he already knows the answer. Like he's already heard it in the way my breath caught, in the way my fingers curled around my glass, in the way I let my own words slip through my teeth.

I swallow.

Hard.

The temperature in the cabin climbs.

Laurent watches me like he's waiting for me to break.

Carter watches me like he's waiting for me to run.

And Hale-

Hale watches me like he already knows I won't do either.

Hale, who hasn't moved, hasn't spoken, hasn't shifted an inch, but whose presence is now thundering through me, sinking into my skin, curling around my spine.

I should leave.

I should let this moment end before it spirals into something I can't escape. But I don't. because if they think they can push me, test me, unravel me first-

They are mistaken.

I inhale, slow and steady as I let the silence stretch just a fraction longer.

Then, with deliberate ease, I lift my glass, rolling the last sip of whiskey across my tongue before setting it down.

And I meet their stares head-on.

Then I say, smooth and devastating,

'That depends... do you like the slow thrill of the descent, or do you prefer the kind of fall you never recover from?'

The air shatters.

The heat erupts.

Laurent's smirk falters, just slightly, his hand flexing against his knee, his gaze trailing lower, darker.

Carter exhales through his nose, his jaw tightening, his fingers pressing into the arms of his chair.

And Hale-

Hale doesn't react.

Doesn't move.

Doesn't blink.

But his eyes change.

Something flickers there, something raw, something deep, something that tells me I just gave him exactly what he wanted.

Something that tells me I should be very, very careful.

I don't breathe.

I don't let them see the way my pulse is pounding, the way my skin feels too hot, too sensitive.

Instead, I rise slowly, smoothly, like none of this has touched me. Like I'm not already burning alive.

And I walk away.

Not quickly. Not hurried.

Measured. Controlled. Completely unaffected.

Even though I know they're watching me go.

Even though I can feel the weight of their stares pressing into my back, searing into my skin, scorching every inch of me.

And the worst part?

I want them to.

I disappear into the galley, the door sliding shut behind me.

Only then - only when I'm alone, away from their eyes,

away from the impossible heat of them-
    Do I let out the breath I didn't realise I was holding.
    Because I just walked away from an inferno.
    But I know I'll be stepping back into it soon enough.
    And next time…
    I don't think they'll let me escape so easily.

*

CHAPTER THREE

The galley is quiet.

Too quiet.

I lean against the cool counter, fingers curled around the edge, pressing down like it'll steady me, ground me, pull me back from the slow burn still creeping beneath my skin.

The door is closed. The men are in the cabin. I am alone.

And yet-

I can still feel them.

Carter's sharp, assessing stare.

Laurent's slow, hungry smirk.

Hale's unshaken stillness - the way his words still echo inside me, low and certain.

I exhale, slow and measured, forcing air back into my lungs, forcing my pulse to settle.

I should feel victorious.

I should feel like I won that exchange.

I should feel like I left them burning, left them speechless, left them thinking about me just as much as I-

I close my eyes.

No.

Don't go there.

I shake my head, reaching for a water bottle, twisting the cap harder than necessary. A distraction. A reset. Anything to cool the fire still licking beneath my ribs.

I take a long sip, the cool liquid doing little to help.

Then the door slides open.

I freeze, my fingers tightening around the bottle.

One of them.

It has to be.

Laurent, stepping inside to push me a little further.

Carter, coming to test me with some new cutting remark.

Hale, saying one sentence too many, pulling me deeper than I should go.

I brace myself, already smoothing my face into something poised, unreadable, untouchable.

And then-

'You look like you've been in the lion's den.'

The breath I was holding releases all at once.

It's not them.

It's Callum.

Our co-pilot stands just inside the doorway, one brow lifted, smirking in that way that makes me instantly suspicious.

Does he know? Did they say something? Did he-

I school my expression, forcing a light laugh. 'Excuse me?'

Callum steps further inside, reaching for a coffee pod from the machine, taking his sweet time. 'I've been in cockpits long enough to recognise turbulence when I see it.'

I cross my arms, forcing my voice into something casual. 'Turbulence?'

He hums, turning the pod over in his hand, like he's

debating how much he wants to say.

Then, after a moment - he looks at me.

Really looks at me.

Like he's already seen too much.

Like he knows.

Then he laughs.

'Any chance of some lunch?'

I pale. 'Oh shit, I'm sorry,' I say as I see the time.

Callum shakes his head, slow and judgmental, still laughing. 'I could only listen to Reynold's complaining for so long.'

'I lost track of time,' I say.

'Watch yourself out there, Quinn,' his smirk deepens as he pops the coffee into the machine, hitting the button. The hum of brewing fills the silence between us.

And then - just loud enough to make my stomach tighten-

'Some men like the chase.'

A slow prickle curls up my spine.

I swallow.

Hard.

'Is that so?' I manage, keeping my voice light.

Callum exhales through his nose, shaking his head slightly, his grin amused but knowing. Like he's already decided how this plays out.

The coffee machine beeps. He grabs his cup, gives me one last glance.

Then he walks out.

Leaving me standing there.

Still too warm.

Still too shaken.

Still wondering if I should have run when I had the chance.

I'm fine.

I smooth my hands down the front of my uniform, straighten my scarf, force my breath to steady. But I can still feel the heat of them. The weight of their stares. The silence I left behind.

I am fine.

I adjust my posture, roll back my shoulders, force my spine to stay straight and strong.

Then I inhale.

Once.

Twice.

I exhale slowly, pressing my palms against the cool countertop.

The galley is small, compact, its stainless steel surfaces gleaming under the soft cabin lights. Everything is perfectly arranged, perfectly in place. It should calm me. The order, the precision. The ritual of control.

But my hands still tremble.

I curl my fingers into fists, willing the sensation away, then reach for the plated meals waiting in the warmer. Focus. That's all I have to do. One step at a time.

Steak for Reynolds, medium rare. Chicken for Callum, paired with steamed asparagus, a delicate lemon butter sauce drizzled over the top.

The motions come easy. Muscle memory. A brush of garnish, a final adjustment, the silverware set just so.

But beneath the meticulousness, the heat won't fade.

It's still there. A deep, low pulse thrumming through me. Relentless. Unshakable.

Because I can still hear Callum's words curling around my spine, dark and edged in knowing amusement.

Some men like the chase.

I swallow, but my throat is dry.

I'm fine.

I reach for a cloth, wiping a perfectly clean surface, needing the movement, needing the distraction. My mind fights against it, dragging me back to the cabin, to the three of them sitting just beyond this partition.

I picture how they're seated.

Carter, lounging like he owns the world, fingers toying absently with the rim of his whiskey glass. Hale, silent and watchful, gaze heavy, arms folded like he's waiting for something inevitable. And Laurent - always smirking, always one step ahead, always the most dangerous because he doesn't just see through me. He enjoys that I let him.

I shiver, my grip tightening on the cloth.

This is madness.

I need to get it together.

I have to get it together.

I draw in another breath, sharper this time, and straighten. I smooth my uniform, adjusting the hem of my skirt, tugging at the edge of my sleeves. My thighs press together instinctively.

A mistake.

Because all it does is remind me.

I suppress a curse and turn back to the tray, sliding each plate into place with precise movements, securing them for the short walk to the cockpit. A simple task.

A simple task that shouldn't feel like a battle.

But as I reach for the tray, my hands still aren't steady.

And worst of all - I don't know if it's from lingering shame...

Or sheer, breathless anticipation.

*

The air changes the second I step out of the galley.

I feel it immediately - the shift, the weight of their eyes, the unspoken charge that lingers in the space between us. I don't look at them. I can't. Not now. Not when every cell in my body is screaming that they're watching me, following me, tracking me.

Hale. Carter. Laurent.

I hear the rustle of fabric as one of them shifts in their seat. The low scrape of a glass against the table. A slow inhale, measured and deep.

My pulse thunders.

But I don't let it show.

I walk. Steady. Controlled. The tray balanced effortlessly in my hands, my grip light, casual. As if my entire body isn't buzzing, as if I don't feel them like a storm gathering at my back.

The carpeted aisle muffles my steps, the cabin unnervingly quiet. The kind of quiet that isn't just absence of sound - but presence. Expectation.

I reach the cockpit door.

Still, I don't look at them.

I raise my knuckles, knuckles that should be steady, and knock.

Tap. Tap. Tap.

I wait.

A pause.

Then- a soft click as the latch disengages.

The door eases open, and I step inside, sealing it behind me, locking the space out - locking them out.

Warm air, low murmuring voices, the steady hum of the controls.

A reset. A moment to gather myself.

I am not affected.

I am composed.

I am fine.

When I turn around, my mask is in place, smooth and unreadable.

Reynolds is still focused on the instruments, scanning the displays.

But Callum-

Callum is already watching me.

His brows lift slightly, a flicker of amusement crossing his face.

Not smug.

Not taunting.

Just knowing.

'Quinn,' he greets, easy, familiar.

I ignore the way my chest tightens.

Instead, I step forward, setting the tray onto the small ledge beside them.

'Lunch,' I announce smoothly. 'Steak for you, Captain. Medium rare, as requested.'

Reynolds nods once, barely glancing up. 'About time.'

I shift, sliding the second plate toward Callum.

'And chicken for you,' I say.

Callum doesn't reach for it right away. Instead, he leans back in his seat, studying me like he's deciding whether or not to say something. Then- he says it anyway.

'You look a little flushed,' he muses, too casual, too light.

I force my expression to stay neutral.

'It's warm in here,' I reply, adjusting the scarf at my throat. 'Small space.'

Callum hums, reaching for his fork. 'So's the cabin.'

My breath catches.

Not enough for him to notice.

But enough for me to feel it.

He doesn't push further.

Doesn't smirk.

Doesn't gloat.

He just picks up his knife, cutting into his chicken with perfect ease.

'Thanks for lunch, Quinn,' he murmurs, like he hasn't just sent heat curling through my stomach.

I nod once, tightly.

Then I turn and leave.

The moment the door clicks shut behind me, I let out the breath I didn't realise I was holding.

My pulse is still too fast.

My skin is still too warm.

But now I have to walk through the cabin again.

Through them.

*

I exhale sharply, pressing my hands against my uniform, as if smoothing out invisible wrinkles might also smooth out the heat still licking beneath my skin.

God help me.

I need a second.

Just a second.

Instead, I keep moving.

One foot in front of the other, forcing my stride to stay smooth, my breath to stay steady.

The galley is my destination. It's safe there.

I just need to make it back.

But as I step back into the main cabin, the air shifts.

Not with silence.

Not with waiting.

But with something worse.

Conversation.

They're talking again. As if nothing happened.

The same sharp, intelligent, heated debate as before.

And yet-

I feel it.

Underneath.

Woven between their words.

The fact that they know I'm here.

That they're aware of me without even acknowledging me.
I keep moving, forcing myself to ignore it.
I will not look.
I will not let them see me falter.
I hear Laurent first, his voice light, easy, too effortless.

'The thing about control is that no one actually wants it,' he muses, stretching in his seat, his words floating through the air like silk. 'They just want the illusion of it.'

Carter exhales sharply, the sound close to a scoff. 'That's naive.'

'No, it's honest,' Laurent counters, amused. 'People don't want to be in control, they just want to be led in the right way.'

'That's manipulation,' Carter replies coolly.

Laurent grins. 'No, that's seduction.'

I inhale sharply, keeping my steps even.
I will not react.
I will not look.

'It's the same thing in business,' Carter continues, his voice level but sharp. 'If you have to convince someone to follow you, you're already losing. The key is making them *want* to follow. To make them believe it was their choice all along.'

'That's assuming they don't know they're being led,' Hale finally speaks, his voice smooth, measured. 'Some people are very aware of what they're walking into.'

My stomach tightens.
I keep my eyes forward.
The galley is just a few more steps away.

I can feel the warmth of their voices wrapping around me, pulling at me, teasing me without ever once speaking my name.

I will not look.
I will not-
My gaze betrays me.

At the last second- at the very moment I reach the edge of the cabin-

I falter.

Just for a fraction of a second.

Just for a heartbeat.

And Laurent catches me.

His head tilts, his smirk spreading slow and devastating as he meets my gaze like he's been waiting for it. Carter's stare flicks to me next, cool and unreadable - but sharp, dissecting, like he's clocked my every breath.

And Hale-

Hale doesn't react.

Doesn't smirk.

Doesn't shift.

He just watches me.

Like he already knew I'd look.

Like he was *waiting* for it.

My breath catches.

Heat pricks up my spine.

I tear my gaze away, forcing myself forward.

I barely make it through the galley door, barely hear it slide closed behind me.

But I already know.

They saw.

And worse-

They *liked* it.

*

I press my hands against the cool marble countertop, curling my fingers over the edge, as if grounding myself might pull the heat from my skin.

I am fine.

I am composed.

But my breath is shallow, my pulse too fast, my body too aware of what just happened. That single moment where I let my gaze slip. Where they saw me falter.

I squeeze my eyes shut, inhale deeply, steady myself-

And the door slides open.

A warm shiver trails down my spine. My fingers press harder into the counter, my breath catching in my throat, but I don't turn right away. I already know who it is.

Carter.

He leans in the doorway, arms crossed, his posture deceptively relaxed, though his eyes tell another story. He watches me like he is waiting for something. Not impatient, not demanding, just... expectant.

I stare at the marble countertop as if it might give me strength. But the moment stretches, and I know I can't pretend I don't feel him there, the weight of his presence coiling around me like a velvet rope.

Finally, he exhales. A slow, measured sound.

'You okay?'

It's soft, careful, but there's something in the way he asks that makes my stomach tighten.

I straighten, smoothing the fabric of my uniform with a quick flick of my hands before lifting my chin. 'Of course,' I say, my voice crisp, polished, in control. 'Why wouldn't I be?'

Carter makes a quiet sound, something close to amusement but heavier. 'No reason.'

He doesn't move, doesn't push. But he also doesn't leave.

I should. I should walk past him, brush it off, keep my distance. But something about the way he looks at me makes my feet stay planted, my breath turn shallow.

I force a small exhale, feigning amusement. 'Is that all? You just came to check on me?'

His lips twitch slightly. 'I was curious.'

'About what?'

'You,' he says simply. 'The way you left, or rather - hurried through.'

My pulse stutters. 'I was delivering lunch to the pilots.'

Carter tilts his head. 'Right,' his gaze flicks downward, a slow drag over my uniform, my hands, the way my fingers grip the counter. When he lifts his eyes back to mine, there's a knowing gleam in them. 'And that's all it was?'

I fold my arms, steadying myself. 'Yes. That's all it was.'

Silence settles between us.

Thick.

Charged.

Carter lets it stretch, lets me feel the weight of it, the pull between us that neither of us has acknowledged out loud.

Then, just when I think he might let me go, he takes a single step forward.

My breath locks in my throat.

It's barely a shift, just enough to make me feel the heat of him, to make my stomach tighten with something sharp and aching.

'I don't believe you,' he murmurs.

His voice is lower now, rougher, as if the control he wears so well is starting to slip.

A shiver rolls through me.

I should scoff, roll my eyes, give some flippant response to break the tension. But I don't. Because my body is betraying me, my breath coming too fast, my pulse a heavy drumbeat in my throat.

He lifts a hand, slow, deliberate, testing the moment. He doesn't touch me. Not yet. Just lets his fingers hover near my hip, so close I can feel the warmth of his skin.

'Quinn,' he murmurs.

My name shouldn't sound like that. Like something dark, something decadent, something he is savouring.

I swallow hard, voice quivering. 'Mr. Carter.'

His lips press together, not quite a smile, not quite a smirk. 'That's not what you were calling me in your head just now.'

Heat flares low in my stomach.

I open my mouth, but before I can say anything, before I can form the words to pull myself back from this ledge, he moves closer.

Not enough to trap me. Still not enough to touch. But enough that I feel surrounded.

My breath shudders out.

He lifts a hand again, this time trailing the back of his knuckles along the side of my jaw. It's the barest touch, a whisper of contact, but it sends a hot, electric shiver down my spine.

I inhale sharply.

He watches me, his gaze dark and unreadable. He slides his fingers higher, fingertips ghosting just beneath my ear, skimming over my pulse, testing the frantic rhythm there.

'I like watching you try not to react,' he murmurs.

I let out a shaky breath. 'I don't know what you're talking about.'

Carter hums, his thumb brushing the edge of my jaw, a single stroke of heat. 'I think you do.'

My hands clench at my sides, aching to push him away, aching to pull him closer.

He tilts his head, studying me with that impossible calm. But I can see the restraint in his posture, the way his chest moves just a fraction deeper as he breathes.

He is holding himself back.

For now.

And I am barely holding myself together.

'You're thinking about it,' he says softly.

'Thinking about what?'

Carter's gaze flicks to my lips. Just for a moment. Just enough.

'You tell me,' he says.

I exhale unsteadily.

His hand cups my jaw, fingers spreading lightly along the side of my throat. Not tight. Not forceful. Just a quiet possession, a touch that holds all the weight of a decision I haven't made yet.

I could step away. I should.

But I don't.

Because I *want* this.

I want him.

He watches me, waiting, letting the silence press between us, letting me sit in the tension of it, letting me feel the moment stretch until it is unbearable.

I should stop this.

I don't.

Instead, I tilt my chin ever so slightly, just enough to meet him halfway.

He doesn't hesitate.

His lips crash into mine.

It isn't careful. It isn't patient. It is heat and hunger, control and surrender, a deliberate, devastating kind of kiss that doesn't ask permission.

It claims.

It *consumes*.

A sound escapes my throat, something desperate, something unfiltered, as his other hand grips my waist and pulls me flush against him.

The counter digs into my back, but I don't care.

All I care about is the way his mouth moves against mine, the way his tongue teases the seam of my lips before I let him in, the way his fingers flex against my waist, branding me with the heat of him.

I clutch at his shirt, nails digging into the fabric, into the hard muscle beneath.

He groans, the sound rough and wrecked, like I just undid him completely.

His hand slides lower, fingers pressing into my hip, pulling me tighter, aligning us in a way that makes me gasp into his mouth.

He exhales sharply, his breath hot against my lips.

'*We shouldn't do this,*' I whisper, but I don't stop him.

He lets out a low, knowing laugh, dragging his lips along my jaw, down my throat.

'Then stop me,' he murmurs against my skin.

I don't.

I won't.

Because I don't want him to stop.

And he knows.

So instead, he *takes*.

And I let him.

I let him.

*

The sound of metal against metal seems deafening above the hum of the aircraft.

A quiet, measured clink.

The soft rustle of leather, slipping through loops, pulling free. The whisper of fabric, the controlled shift of movement behind me, the tension coiling tighter.

I squeeze my eyes shut, my breath shuddering out of me as the reality crashes in all at once - there's no stopping this now.

I don't *want* to stop.

He turns me, braces me against the cool marble, my fingers curling over the edge, as his hands return to me.

Slow.

Teasing.

Possessive.

He slides them beneath my skirt, dragging his palms up my thighs, spanning them, feeling the heat of my skin, his fingers pressing in, spreading, claiming.

I tremble.

He hums, low, dark, satisfied.

'So needy,' he murmurs, his lips brushing my nape, his breath warm and taunting, his body a wall of heat at my back.

My pulse pounds between my ribs, between my thighs, everywhere he touches me, everywhere he hasn't touched me yet.

Then his fingers hook beneath my panties.

A sharp inhale.

A soft, silken slip.

Down.

Away.

The air kisses my bare skin, the coolness a stark contrast to the heat pooling between my thighs, to the deep, slow burn growing unbearably inside me.

I shift, pressing closer to the counter, my body trembling with want, with anticipation, with the knowledge that he is about to ruin me.

He groans, low, guttural, his hands spanning my hips, pulling me back into him, his fingers pressing into the softness of my skin.

'I should make you beg for it,' he rasps, his mouth dragging along my jaw, his teeth scraping gently.

I whimper.

Because I would.

I already am.

I'm shaking for him, melting for him, lost in the storm of him.

But there's no teasing left.

No slow game.

No drawn-out seduction.

Because he wants this as much as I do.

Because he's just as desperate.

Because he's already pulling me forward, lifting me just enough, positioning me exactly where he wants me.

I brace-

Then-

The first brush of him.

Bare.

Thick.

Hot.

My breath shatters, my entire body arching, trembling, opening for him.

'Quinn…' he breathes, his voice raw, reverent, aching with restraint.

Like he's fighting himself.

Like he's on the edge of losing control.

Like he's about to fall.

And so am I.

He slides forward, nudging my pussy, pressing, a slow, torturous glide, stretching the moment, making me feel every inch of him, teasing me with what's coming.

I grip the counter harder, my nails biting into the marble, my body burning from the inside out.

And then-

His cock sinks into me.

Deep.

Exquisite.

A long, slow, aching stretch, filling me completely, taking everything I give him, giving me everything in return.

A sharp gasp tears from my lips, my spine arching, curving, pressing me further into him.

'*God*, Quinn…' his voice is hoarse, ruined, his hands gripping my hips, his fingers pressing into my skin like he can't hold himself back.

I moan, my body clenching, pulling him deeper, the pleasure shocking, overwhelming, my head tipping forward, my breath coming in broken gasps.

He stills for a moment, his chest rising and falling hard against my back, his fingers sliding up my arms, curling over my hands where I grip the counter, twining our fingers together.

Intimate.

Tender.

Desperate.

I feel every inch of his thick cock inside of me, every pulse, every twitch, the weight of him, the press of his chest at my back, the heat of his lips at my temple.

'Is this what you wanted?' he murmurs, his voice softer now, lower, thick with something deep and unspoken.

I shudder.

Because yes.

God, yes.

This - this is what I wanted.

What I *needed*.

I press back into him, taking him deeper, a moan slipping from my lips as I surrender completely.

'*Yes*,' I whisper.

And Carter moves.

Slow.

Deep.

Unrelenting.

His fingers stay tangled with mine, holding me there, keeping me grounded even as he takes me apart.

And I let him.

I let him pull me under.

I let him make me *his*.

He moves, and the world narrows to the slow, deep push

of him inside me.

I feel everything.

The way his thick cock fills me, stretches me, claims me with every careful stroke. The way his breath hitches at my ear, each exhale ragged, controlled but barely.

I bite down on my lip, my nails digging into the marble, my body trembling, tightening, my breath coming in sharp little gasps as I try - *try* - to stay quiet.

But I'm losing that fight.

The tension builds, the pleasure coiling tighter, his movements slow and relentless, pulling out, leaving me aching, empty - only to sink back in, deeper, hotter, heavier.

I choke on a moan, my lips parting soundlessly, my fingers gripping his hands where he still has them locked over mine.

His grip tightens, like he can feel me slipping, like he can sense the way I'm about to shatter apart for him.

'*Quinn…*'

His voice is a rasp, low and ruined, and the way he says my name sends another shudder rolling through me, my body clenching, pulling him deeper.

I feel him everywhere.

The hard press of his chest at my back, the warmth of his breath against my neck, the silken slide of his mouth along my jaw.

And, *God* - his hands.

One still holding mine in place, our fingers laced, pinning me there like he needs me to know I'm his. The other sliding lower, teasing over my stomach, dipping beneath the fabric of my blouse, his fingers brushing against bare skin, stroking, finding my nipple, soothing, claiming.

I whimper, the sound muffled, strangled, but not enough.

Because he hears it.

Because his hips flex just a little sharper, because his teeth graze my earlobe, because his breath turns rougher, hotter, needier.

I try to keep it in, to bite down on the sound, but the trying only makes it worse - only makes the pleasure sharper, higher, closer.

'Let me hear you,' he murmurs, his voice thick and commanding, his hand skimming lower, teasing, taunting, coaxing me closer to the edge.

I shake my head, my teeth sinking into my bottom lip, desperate to hold back, to keep from breaking completely.

But Carter knows.

He knows I'm losing control.

He knows I want to fall.

His movements quicken, each deep, perfect stroke building, layering, pushing me closer, the heat pulsing, the pleasure breaking apart inside me.

I shake, my body arching, my legs trembling, my breath coming in desperate, ragged little gasps.

And then-

The pleasure crashes through me, sharp and shattering, a wild, helpless cry tearing from my lips before I can stop it.

He groans, deep and guttural, his grip tightening as he thrusts once, *twice-*

And I *feel* him.

A shuddering exhale, a hard tremor, his entire body tensing, tightening, releasing.

I feel every pulse of him, every twitch, every throb, every quake as he spills into me, his chest rising and falling in sharp, uneven bursts, his lips pressed to my shoulder, his breath hot and wrecked against my skin as his love overwhelms me.

My knees give out, my body collapsing against the counter, and he catches me, holding me up, his arms strong, steady, unyielding as he keeps me from falling apart completely.

We breathe together, our heartbeats wild, erratic, matching

each other beat for beat.

The cabin is quiet, the air thick with the scent of him, of me, of us, of what we've just done.

And Carter - Carter just stays there, pressed against my back, his arms still wrapped around me, his lips still grazing my shoulder, his fingers still tangled with mine.

As if he's not ready to let go yet.

As if he never wants to let go at all.

*

CHAPTER FOUR

The heat lingers between us, thick and smoldering. The quiet hum of the aircraft seems impossibly distant, swallowed by the pulse of my own heartbeat, by the steady, ragged breaths Carter exhales against my skin.

He doesn't move.

Neither do I.

We stay like this, bodies entwined, his weight grounding me, his warmth wrapping around me, the aftershocks still rippling through both of us. The slow, pulsing throb of him still buried deep inside me, the lingering tremors in my thighs, the way my body clenches instinctively around him, not ready to let him go.

And Carter feels it too.

His fingers flex against my waist, tightening just enough to send another sharp spark of awareness through me. His breath fans against the nape of my neck, warm and uneven, and then I feel it - his lips, the softest graze, just barely there, as if he's savouring the taste of my skin.

A shiver rolls through me.

He hums low, pleased, his hands smoothing down over my hips, slow and possessive. He shifts slightly behind me, not enough to pull away, just enough to make me feel the movement, the subtle friction, the still-sensitive ache between my legs sparking with new life.

I suck in a breath.

And he smiles.

I can feel it against my skin, the slight upward curve of his lips as he presses another slow, lingering kiss to my shoulder. Then, he whispers, his voice low, husky, deliberate.

'You're still hungry for me.'

A pulse of pure heat jolts through me, my body betraying me, my breath catching in my throat as I feel myself clench around him again.

He groans softly, a quiet, knowing sound, his fingers tightening on my hips, his chest pressing closer to my back.

'I can feel it, Quinn,' he murmurs. 'The way you don't want me to move. The way you don't want me to leave you empty.'

I exhale sharply, my fingers gripping the counter as a fresh wave of need crashes through me, sudden, uncontrollable.

Because he's right.

God, he's right.

But as I tremble in his hold, something stirs deeper still

A low ache that hasn't faded, even after he has taken me, even after I have unraveled in his arms. It is still there, thrumming beneath the surface, insatiable, burning hotter instead of cooling.

I should be satisfied.

But I'm not.

It isn't enough.

Carter alone isn't enough.

The realization crashes through me - sharp, overwhelming, undeniable.

Because I want more.

More than just him.

More than just this.

More than I have ever dared to admit.

The thought shakes me, makes my breath catch in my throat, makes my fingers tighten against the cool marble like I need to hold onto something, like I need an anchor to stop myself from slipping deeper into this new, terrifying, undeniable hunger.

Carter notices.

He stills against me, his fingers flexing, his breath a fraction sharper.

Then, slowly, deliberately, he trails his lips along the curve of my jaw, his voice a deep, knowing murmur.

'Tell me what you're thinking.'

I press my lips together, forcing myself to breathe, to steady the sudden, dizzying rush of need coursing through me.

'I don't know,' I whisper, but it is a lie.

Carter makes a quiet, thoughtful sound. His hand slides over my stomach, down my thigh, his fingers teasing, testing, coaxing.

'Yes, you do,' he murmurs.

My breath shudders.

Because I do.

God, I do.

But I don't know how to say it.

How to tell him that my body is still aching, that something inside me has been unlocked and I don't know how to close it again. That what I felt with him, as deep and consuming as it was, has only made me crave more.

More hands.

More mouths.

More bodies pressing into mine.

More.

He exhales against my skin, slow and considering. His grip on my hips tightens, like he is testing a theory, like he already knows the answer.

'It wasn't enough, was it?'

I inhale sharply, my pulse hammering at the truth in his words.

He turns my head slightly, just enough to meet my eyes, his gaze dark and knowing. His lips brush the corner of my mouth, teasing, not quite a kiss.

'I felt it,' he murmurs. 'The way you were still searching. The way your body didn't want to stop.'

I shudder, my skin heating, my thighs pressing together as another wave of need pulses through me. He smiles again, slow and wicked, his fingers skimming lower, teasing the place where we are still joined, still pulsing together.

'You want more.'

I make a strangled sound, my breath hitching, my body arching instinctively into his touch.

Carter groans softly, tilting his head, his lips grazing my ear.

'You're so greedy,' he murmurs, the words soft but devastating. 'Still trembling, still clenching around me, still aching for more when I've already given you everything.'

My entire body flushes, heat rolling down my spine, pooling low in my belly, sharp and restless and impossible to ignore.

'I-'

'Look at you.' Carter presses a lazy, indulgent kiss to my shoulder, his hands gliding over my skin like he owns me, like he knows exactly what I need. 'Still shaking. Still dripping. Still desperate.'

A low whimper slips from my throat, my head tipping back, my pulse hammering against my ribs. Carter hums, his lips grazing the shell of my ear, his fingers sliding lower, testing, teasing.

'It's almost like you can't be satisfied,' he whispers, voice laced with quiet amusement, with something darker, something knowing. 'Like no matter how much I give you, it will never be enough.'

A violent shiver rolls through me, my knees going weak beneath the sheer, brutal truth of it.

He chuckles, soft and low, his grip steadying me, keeping me upright, keeping me exactly where he wants me.

'That's it, isn't it?' he muses, voice dripping with wicked satisfaction. 'You need *more*.'

I squeeze my eyes shut, my breath shuddering, my body betraying me with another sharp pulse of want.

Because I do.

God, I do.

He tilts my chin up, forcing me to meet his gaze, his own eyes dark and steady, filled with something deep and burning.

'How bad do you need it, Quinn?'

The words scrape over my skin, ignite something helpless inside me, something I don't know how to contain.

I swallow hard, my lips parting, but no sound comes out.

He watches me struggle, his smile turning just a little sharper, just a little crueler. Then, he leans in close, his breath hot against my ear.

'We both know you're not done.'

The words hit me like a slow, deliberate spark, sending a fresh wave of heat spiraling through me, setting something alight inside me that I don't know how to put out.

Because he's right.

I'm not done.

But before I can open my mouth, before I can tell him *exactly* how much I still need, the quietest sound slips through the cabin beyond the door.

A footstep.

A shift of movement.

Someone is close.

Carter hears it at the same time I do. His body tenses, his grip still firm around me, but his expression doesn't change - not even an inch.

God. He's so composed. So calm, so smooth, even after taking me apart completely.

I, on the other hand, am still pulsing, still undone, still aching with need.

A slow smile curves against his lips as his hand drags down my thigh, his touch lingering as he leans in just close enough for his breath to ghost over my skin.

'You should fix your uniform,' he murmurs, all deep satisfaction and wicked amusement.

I bite my lip hard, swallowing down the sharp pulse of heat that his words send through me.

He's right.

I need to pull myself together before I step out of this galley.

Before I face the rest of them.

Before I let them see just how wrecked I still am from Carter's hands.

But as he steps back, as he tucks himself away and smooths down his own clothes like nothing just happened, I feel it coil even deeper inside me-

This isn't enough.

Not yet.

I do want more.

And I have two more men waiting in that cabin.

* * *

*

The lavatory is too bright.

Harsh, clinical light spills from the mirror, too sharp, too revealing, showing me exactly what I don't want to see - flushed skin, swollen lips, the lingering, unmistakable heat still clinging to my body.

I grip the edge of the small sink, my breath still uneven, too shallow, too fast.

What the hell am I doing?

This isn't me. This has *never* been me. I don't *do* this. I don't blur the lines. I don't lose myself in the space between professionalism and recklessness. I've spent years holding myself together, keeping the uniform crisp, the lines clear, the power in my own hands.

I *know* how to navigate men like them.

And yet- I let Carter have me.

The realisation hits like a jolt to my system. Not because I regret it. *God, no.* That's the problem. I *don't* regret it. At all. I can still feel him - the way his hands claimed me, the way his mouth burned against my skin, the way I let go, let him take, let myself be taken.

A shiver rolls through me.

I don't recognise the me in the mirror.

She looks… *different*.

Looser. Wilder. Like something has cracked open inside of her, something deep and aching and unsatisfied. I swallow hard, pressing a palm against my stomach, as if I can push it all back down.

It's done. It's over.

But it doesn't *feel* over.

Because I'm still shaking. Still too warm, still too hungry, still aching for more.

I drag in a breath and turn on the faucet, letting the water rush cool over my hands before I cup a handful and press it to my face. The cold bites against my skin, grounding me for a brief, sharp moment.

Breathe.

I inhale deeply, counting the seconds before I exhale. Again. Again. Steady. Controlled.

Except it isn't.

Because this wasn't enough. Carter wasn't enough. One moment, one stolen, reckless act wasn't enough to quiet the hunger that's still clawing at me from the inside.

I grip the edges of the sink harder, knuckles white.

This is dangerous.

I know it. I should pull back. I should get out of here, return to the cabin, pretend like I can step back from the edge before I fall. But the truth is I've already fallen.

And as I meet my own gaze in the mirror - dark, heavy - lidded, pulse still pounding in my throat - I know exactly what's coming next.

Because Carter's waiting for me.

They all are.

The cold water drips from my chin as I brace my hands on the sink, breath shaky, uneven.

I can still feel him.

Carter.

His hands on my skin. His mouth at my throat. His body caging me in, wrecking me, ruining me. I should feel ashamed. I should feel remorse. I should be questioning everything.

Instead, I want more.

I drag in another breath, my reflection staring back at me, cheeks flushed, lips swollen, pupils blown wide with lingering hunger.

I look like I've been taken.

I look like I've been claimed.

Because I *have*.

I press my thighs together, as if that will stop the pulse of heat, as if that will quiet the hunger still curling deep inside me.

It doesn't.

God, it doesn't.

I inhale sharply, straighten my uniform, force myself to breathe.

'Fuck.'

I press the button to open door.

And I step straight into him.

Hale.

Tall. Silent. Waiting.

I freeze.

He doesn't move. Doesn't say a word. He just watches. Drinks me in. Slow. Excruciating. His eyes start at mine, pinning me in place, burning right through me.

Then they drop.

Oh.

He sees it. All of it. The way my uniform is just slightly rumpled. The way my pulse jumps in my throat. The way I'm still shaking, still wrecked, still not recovered.

Heat pools low in my stomach, dark and hot and needy.

Because he knows.

He knows exactly what I've been doing. He knows how Carter just had me. And he's imagining it. I can see it in the slow way his gaze moves over me, tracking every inch of my body, lingering at my mouth, at my throat, at the places Carter's hands have just been.

I should say something.

I should move.

I should do *anything* but stand here, melting under the weight of his stare.

But I don't.

I just stand, breathless, burning, waiting. And for a moment, I think he's going to take me too.

Right here.

Right now.

Right up against this door.

And God help me, I would let him.

I would let him grab me, push me back inside, shut the door and ruin me all over again. I would let him devour me. I see it in his eyes - the dark flicker of restraint, the edge of control that he's holding onto by a thread. And I think - if I make one sound, if I reach for him, if I so much as breathe the wrong way... he'll snap.

But he doesn't.

Instead, he moves.

Not toward me.

Not to claim me.

He steps aside. He lets me go. And that - *that* - is somehow so much worse.

My body thrums, my skin flushes, my thighs clench as I force myself to walk past him. Every step is agony. Because I can feel his eyes on me. Feel the heat, the weight, the hunger he's not acting on.

Not yet.

I don't breathe again until I'm down the hall. Even then - I'm still trembling.

I walk carefully. One foot in front of the other. Chin high. Shoulders back. Nothing shaken. Nothing out of place. At least, that's what I tell myself.

The cabin is quieter now. More relaxed. The hush of indulgence, the kind of ease that only comes when men like them have had their fill of whiskey and conversation. As I move past them, I hear it. Snippets of low, unfiltered talk.

'You'd have folded in five minutes,' Laurent is saying, amusement rich in his voice. 'Face it, Carter, she had your balls in a vice from the second you sat down.'

A slow, measured sip follows.

'I let her *think* she did,' Carter replies smoothly.

Laurent chuckles. 'Same thing in the end.'

'I disagree,' Carter murmurs. 'Control is perception. Give someone the illusion of it, and you own them completely.'

Laurent makes a sound. Considering. Appreciative.

'You always did have a talent for that.'

I don't listen. Not really. But the words curl around me as I pass, seeping into my skin.

Control is perception.

I swallow. I tell myself not to look.

But then-

Carter's gaze lifts to mine.

And I falter.

Just for a second.

Just enough.

A flicker of something - something dangerous, something intimate - shifts between us. It's different now. Before, he was all power, all dominance, all command. But now, he knows something.

He knows the way my breath hitched against his mouth. He knows the way my body melted beneath his hands. He knows exactly how I fell apart for him.

And he's still thinking about it.

The corner of his mouth twitches, the faintest curve - so small, so barely there, it feels like a secret. Like a brand pressed into my skin. Heat blooms low and deep.

I should keep walking. I should breathe. But Laurent is watching now too. His gaze flicks from Carter to me, slow and sharp, like he's reading something invisible, something unspoken. Like he's already decided what it means. Then Carter exhales the faintest, almost imperceptible breath through his nose, before-

He looks away.

Laurent smirks, dragging a finger over the rim of his glass.

I inhale sharply.

I blink.

And then, as smoothly as I can, I walk on. But it doesn't matter. Because my pulse is still hammering. Because my thighs still clench with the memory of him.

Because Laurent knows.

And I have the sinking feeling he's about to use that knowledge.

I almost make it.

The galley is just ahead, the thin partition of the curtain waiting, the illusion of safety within reach.

But then-

'Quinn?'

Laurent's voice is silk and steel.

I freeze.

Heat surges up my neck as I school my expression, exhaling through my nose before I turn back, composed.

'Yes, Mr Laurent?'

His smile is slow, sharp. 'Be a darling and top me up, won't you?'

Be a darling.

I step back, head toward the bar. My pulse hammers as I approach, hyper-aware of the way Carter hasn't moved, the sheer size of him next to Laurent, his presence dark, potent.

The decanter is almost empty. I reach for it, steady fingers grasping cool glass.

And then-

The barest touch.

A slow, insidious brush of fingertips up the back of my thigh.

Carter.

A soft glide.

Barely there.

But *devastating*.

I suck in a breath, keeping my expression smooth, controlled, as I tip the whiskey into Laurent's glass.

Another stroke.

Higher.

Heat coils through me, twisting deep, pooling between my thighs.

Laurent speaks.

I don't hear him.

Not really.

Because Carter's fingers are moving higher still.

Because my body is betraying me.

Because I *want* it.

A slow, lazy press against the crease beneath my skirt, featherlight, teasing.

I clench my thighs, hard.

Laurent chuckles, swirling his glass, oblivious.

'Good girl,' he murmurs.

The words slide through me.

Carter's fingers curl, just barely pressing.

I almost gasp.

But I don't.

Because I can't.

Because I have to stand here, play the part, pretend I'm not coming undone.

And Carter- he knows.

I feel it in the lazy drag of his touch, in the way his fingers pause, his own silent amusement.

I meet Laurent's eyes, keeping my face carefully blank.

'Will that be all, sir?' I ask, voice smooth.

Laurent's smirk deepens, like he's enjoying something he can't quite name.

'I suspect not,' he says.

And I swallow.

Because now I have to walk away.

Laurent swirls his whiskey, watching me too closely.

'Tell me, Quinn,' he muses, his voice smooth, indulgent, the edge of something sharper hidden beneath. 'How much access do you have to the aircraft?'

My pulse jumps.

I smooth my expression, ignoring the way Carter's fingertips haven't moved.

'All that I require, sir,' I say, careful, professional.

Laurent hums, tilting his head. 'And if I were to require something... out of the ordinary?'

My grips tightens on the neck of the decanter.

'That would depend, sir.'

Laurent's smile is pure sin.

'Let's say I happened to have something particularly rare and expensive stowed away in the hold. Something *highly* exclusive,' he leans forward just slightly, eyes gleaming. 'Would you be able to retrieve it for me?'

I still.

The cargo hold is off-limits mid-flight.

We all know this.

And yet-

Laurent watches me, testing, waiting to see if I'll play his game.

And Carter- Carter is still touching me.

A slow, deliberate stroke.

Higher.

I exhale sharply, forcing myself to remain impassive. 'I'm afraid that wouldn't be allowed, sir.'

Laurent sighs, his smirk deepening. 'A shame.'

I take a careful step back, but Carter doesn't move his hand right away, the heat of his touch lingering like a brand.

Laurent taps his glass against his knee.

'Tell me, Quinn,' he continues, tone lazy, probing. 'Have you ever bent the rules before?'

My breath catches.

I see the challenge in his gaze, the subtle invitation.

I think of Carter.

Of the way he just had me in the galley.

I think of Hale.

Of the way he looked at me outside the lavatory, the restraint in his dark, brooding eyes.

I think of all the ways I've already broken the rules.

Laurent waits, expectant, his lips curling as mine dry.

Carter's touch lingers, fading too slowly.

I meet Laurent's eyes.

And I lie, smoothly-

'Never, sir.'

His grin widens.

Laurent doesn't react right away. His lips press together in a thoughtful line, eyes gleaming with something dark, something intrigued. He leans back in his seat, fingers idly tracing the rim of his tumbler as if weighing his next move.

I stand my ground, heart hammering, skin still buzzing from the ghost of Carter's touch. I know the power in the word *never* - how it tempts men like Laurent, men who aren't used to being told no. Men who think rules are just suggestions waiting to be rewritten in their favor.

He hums, tapping his glass against the table once. 'Shame. I had something truly rare down there. A once-in-a-lifetime indulgence. But I suppose rules are rules.'

Beside me, Carter shifts, his fingers still barely skimming the back of my thigh, hidden from sight. A quiet, unspoken question. The heat of it lingers, burning through the thin fabric of my stockings.

I keep my expression neutral, but I know exactly what Laurent is doing - pushing, prodding, waiting for the moment I cave.

I tilt my head, let a slow, knowing smile play at my lips. 'Unless, of course, there was an emergency.'

Laurent's gaze sharpens. 'An emergency?'

I nod, dragging out the moment, letting the tension stretch just enough to make him lean in. 'A mechanical fault. A suspected leak. A suspicious noise from below deck. Anything that might require the crew to inspect the hold to ensure the safety of the aircraft,' my voice dips, softer, silkier. 'Wouldn't want to put you in harm's way, sir.'

Laurent watches me, the corners of his mouth twitching, not quite a smirk, but close. 'How very diligent of you, Miss Quinn.'

I hold his gaze. 'Safety first.'

Carter exhales a quiet laugh, barely audible over the hum of the aircraft, but I feel it against my skin, feel it in the subtle shift of his fingers before he withdraws his touch entirely, as if relinquishing me to Laurent - for now.

Laurent swirls his drink, eyes glinting with something wicked. 'And if I were to hear something suspicious? Say, in the next few minutes?'

I don't miss a beat. 'Then I'd be obliged to investigate.'

He places his glass down with a decisive clink, fingers steepling as he regards me. 'Then let's hope my ears are sharp.'

Heat licks up my spine. I know exactly what I've just agreed to.

And god help me, I'm already stepping toward the edge of that line, wondering just how much further I'm willing to go.

I step back, slow and measured, not breaking eye contact with Laurent until the last second. My pulse thrums, a hot, heady beat beneath my skin as I turn away, ready to slip back to the galley.

But before I take another step, Carter moves.

Not overtly. Not enough to draw Laurent's attention. Just a small shift in his seat, a slight tilt of his head - an invitation.

It stops me cold.

I know I should keep walking. Keep playing the part of the untouchable flight attendant, composed and professional, unaffected by the heated glances, the brushes of fingers, the sheer gravitational pull of these men.

But Carter…

I turn back to him, letting my hands skim the edge of the leather seat beside him, lingering longer than necessary.

He's watching me with that same unreadable expression, but there's something else in his eyes now - something I recognise.

A challenge.

A temptation.

'Quinn,' his voice is low, a private murmur just for me.

A shiver prickles at the base of my neck.

'I should go,' I whisper, barely audible over the hum of the aircraft.

His fingers twitch on the armrest. 'But you won't.'

He's right. I don't.

Instead, I let my gaze flick down, just once, catching the way his chest rises and falls, the way his hand flexes as though resisting the urge to reach for me.

Then, finally, I look back up at him, tilting my head just slightly. 'You like watching me break the rules, don't you?'

A slow, almost imperceptible smirk tugs at the corner of his mouth. 'I like watching you consider breaking them too.'

I exhale, a soft, unsteady thing that betrays just how much I feel this moment, how tightly wound I am from the weight of his attention.

His hand shifts again, just the smallest movement, like he might - just might - reach for me.

But then-

'Oh dear,' Laurent muses, stretching languidly in his seat. 'I do believe I just heard something quite disconcerting from below deck.'

Carter's expression doesn't change, but something in his posture shifts - his jaw tightens, his fingers curl against the armrest.

I straighten slowly, smoothing my hands down the front of my uniform before turning back to Laurent, once again schooling my features into something neutral, something unaffected.

'Is that so?' I ask, voice deceptively light.

Laurent's grin is all sharp edges. 'Mmm. A most unusual sound. Might need investigating, wouldn't you say?'

A pulse of heat flares low in my stomach.

I glance once more at Carter, our moment shattered but still lingering in the air between us, unresolved. Then, without another word, I turn on my heel and head for the access panel.

Let him follow if he dares.

*

The access panel clicks shut above me, sealing off the world above, leaving me alone in the belly of the plane.

The air is different down here. Colder. Denser. The deep thrumming of the engines is amplified, a constant vibration that hums through the metal walls, rattling through the cargo containers. It smells of leather, steel, and something faintly chemical - the scent of aviation fuel lingering in the confined space.

Dim lighting strips cast long shadows, flickering as I step further inside. The hold is small, a tight stretch of space lined with secured luggage, netting, and reinforced panels. No windows, no luxury, just the raw underbelly of the jet.

My heart pounds, half from exertion, half from anticipation.

I move carefully, my heels clicking against the metal flooring as I weave through the stacked cases, searching for Laurent's bag. He hadn't told me exactly where it was, only that I'd *'know it when I saw it.'*

I take a slow breath, running my fingers along the smooth surface of a designer duffel, then another.

Nothing.

The plane jolts slightly, a shift in altitude that sends a ripple through the hold. I steady myself against a crate, my pulse kicking up another notch. The noise down here is relentless - the deep rumble of the engines, the occasional groan of shifting cargo, the constant awareness of the vast sky pressing in around us.

I'm alone.

Completely and utterly alone.

The thought shouldn't excite me as much as it does.

I spot it then - a case that stands out among the others. Sleek, dark, expensive.

Laurent's taste, undoubtedly.

I crouch beside it, fingertips grazing the monogrammed leather before unfastening the buckles.

Inside, nestled in the folds of silk-lined fabric, is exactly what I expected. A bottle, gleaming in the dim light, the label so decadent it practically purrs luxury. The kind of vintage that isn't sold, only traded among those with power and influence. A forbidden indulgence.

My mouth goes dry.

I know this wasn't just a test of whether I'd break protocol. This was something else.

A lure.

A game.

The engines groan again, and I glance up, a sudden

awareness prickling at my skin.

I'm not alone anymore.

A shadow moves just beyond the stacks of cases.

Carter?

No.

I swallow, fingers tightening around the neck of the bottle as I straighten.

Laurent.

'I didn't think you'd actually come down here yourself,' I murmur, my voice carrying just enough edge to mask the unsteady flutter in my chest.

Laurent steps into the low light, slow and deliberate. His gaze sweeps over me, assessing, amused. 'And yet, here you are. Kneeling in the dark, fingers wrapped around something extremely indulgent.'

His smirk deepens as he closes the distance, his voice low, dark silk against the roar of the engines. 'Tell me, Quinn... do you always obey when a man asks for something forbidden?'

I grip the bottle a little tighter, the weight of it cool and solid in my palm. The flickering lights cast his face in half-shadow, his sharp features all the more cutting in the dimness. The air is thick between us, charged, and I know - I know - that Laurent isn't just here for the champagne.

He moves closer, slow and deliberate, the way a predator prowls in on something soft and unsuspecting. Except I'm not unsuspecting. I feel every shift in the air, every step that shrinks the space between us until the heat of his body grazes mine.

'You didn't answer my question, chérie,' he murmurs, his voice a velvet rasp against the raw hum of the engines. 'Do you always obey when a man asks for something forbidden? Or do you prefer being the one to make the rules?'

I exhale slowly, refusing to step back, refusing to give him the satisfaction. 'I make exceptions,' I say, my voice even, betraying nothing.

His gaze flickers down, following the slow rise and fall of my breath. 'For whom?'

I don't answer. I can't answer. Because we both know what he's asking.

His fingers lift, dragging up my arm in the lightest ghost of a touch, tracing the crisp line of my uniform sleeve. 'I think you like breaking rules, Quinn,' he muses, almost to himself. 'You certainly didn't hesitate coming down here, slipping away into the dark, alone. You must have known I wouldn't let you be alone for long.'

His knuckles skim my jaw, tipping my chin up just a fraction. Not forcing. Just suggesting.

'Unless that's exactly what you wanted.'

My pulse kicks against my ribs.

'I came down here to retrieve this,' I say, lifting the bottle between us, using it as a shield, as a barrier, something solid to hold on to. But Laurent doesn't even glance at it. His eyes stay on me, heavy, knowing.

'And now that you have it?' he asks, his voice dark silk. 'Are you going to return like a good little flight attendant? Or are you going to linger?'

His fingers drift lower, toying with the edge of my collar, his touch searing. He smells expensive, like rare cologne and the sharp bite of whiskey, laced with something richer, something inherently him.

I swallow.

This is dangerous.

This is reckless.

This is exactly what I shouldn't want.

But his breath is warm against my skin, his presence overwhelming.

'Laurent…' I warn, though it doesn't sound like a warning at all.

He smiles. Slow. Satisfied.

'That's better,' he murmurs. 'Say my name again, chérie.'

I don't. I can't.

Because if I do, I might just let him win.

Laurent's smirk deepens, his fingers still idly toying with the edge of my collar, as if he has all the time in the world to unravel me.

'You know, chérie,' he murmurs, voice rich and low, 'I was thinking… since you've already bent the rules for me, it's only fair you pay the price.'

My breath catches.

'Pay the price?' I echo, my voice just a whisper.

His fingers ghost down my throat, barely a touch, but enough to leave a trail of heat in their wake. 'It's only *just*, don't you think? A stewardess who breaks protocol, sneaks away in the dead of flight…' his lips twitch. 'That sort of behavior calls for *discipline*.'

A slow shiver rolls through me, a delicious mix of anticipation and warning.

Laurent is pushing - flirting, yes, but something darker lingers beneath his words, something that makes my skin prickle, my breath turn shallow.

I swallow, trying to ground myself, trying to stay unaffected. 'And what sort of… *discipline* do you imagine for me?'

Laurent exhales a quiet laugh, almost like he's pleased I asked, pleased I didn't shut him down outright. He steps closer still, the space between us now almost nonexistent, the heat of him seeping through my uniform.

'That depends,' he murmurs, eyes gleaming with something wicked. 'Are you the sort of woman who prefers a firm hand? Or do you prefer something slower… something drawn out?'

My thighs squeeze together of their own accord.

I shouldn't be here.

I shouldn't be entertaining this.

'You're trembling,' he notes, tilting his head as if he's truly studying me, like I'm some puzzle he's determined to solve. His fingers trail lower, skimming the bare skin of my wrist. 'Is it fear?'

I open my mouth to deny it, to steady myself, but then his other hand lifts - just the back of his fingers brushing the outside of my thigh where my skirt ends, his touch barely there, but devastating.

A sharp breath escapes me.

He leans in, lips so close to my ear I can feel the heat of his words.

'Or is it something else?'

Laurent's lips barely graze the edge of my ear, his breath warm, intoxicating, each syllable a lure deeper into dangerous territory.

'Is it anticipation, chérie?' he murmurs, voice silk-wrapped sin.

I press my hands to the cool metal beside me, grounding myself, but it does nothing to slow the thundering of my pulse. My uniform suddenly feels too tight, my skin too warm.

His fingers, deliberate and unhurried, skate over the hem of my skirt again, just the barest brush against my thigh. 'I think it is,' he muses, more to himself than me. 'I think you like the idea of it- being caught down here, being at my mercy.'

I exhale sharply, my breath shuddering. 'I-'

'*Shh*,' he presses a single finger to my lips, his eyes dark with amusement, with something far more dangerous. 'No lies, Quinn. Not here.'

He watches me for a reaction, drinking in every flicker of emotion that betrays me.

'Tell me...' he trails his knuckles up my thigh, slow, coaxing, enough to send a helpless shiver through me. 'Would you submit, if I asked you to? Would you take your punishment like a good girl?'

A slow, decadent heat blooms in my core, molten and consuming.

I should shut him down. I should turn, step away, regain control of myself.

Instead, my lips part on a shallow, hitched breath.

Laurent's smirk sharpens, triumphant. 'Ah... I thought so.'

Before I can react, he moves - fast, decisive. His hands find my hips, and in one smooth motion, he turns me, bending me forward over a waist-high crate. A gasp slips from my mouth, my palms pressing against the cool surface for balance.

Heat floods my skin, my breath catching as I feel the solid weight of him just behind me. The cargo hold hums around us, the distant thrum of the engines vibrating through the metal walls, but the sound is nothing compared to the rush of blood in my ears.

Laurent's hands slide deliberately up the backs of my thighs, slow, teasing, mapping me as though he has all the time in the world.

'Mmm... now this,' he murmurs, his palm skimming up the curve of my hip before trailing down my spine in a slow, measured caress, 'is a view worth breaking protocol for.'

I shudder, every nerve alight.

His fingertips graze the hem of my skirt, toying with it, lifting just enough to make my pulse stutter. He's testing me, watching, waiting to see how far I'll let him go.

'Do you know what I love most about this, chérie?' he muses, pressing just a little closer, enough that I feel the heat of his body against mine. 'The way you tremble. You act like you're in control, but here... like this...' his hand slides back up my spine, a slow, deliberate stroke. 'I can feel the truth of it. You want this. You crave it.'

I squeeze my eyes shut, my breath coming faster now, my nails pressing into the crate beneath my hands.

His lips ghost over my ear. 'Say it, Quinn. Tell me you like being held like this… bent over, waiting… wondering what I'll do next.'

A shiver rolls through me, anticipation coiling so tight it's almost unbearable.

I swallow hard. 'I…'

His grip firms just slightly at my hips. 'Go on.'

My body betrays me. I shift instinctively against him, a soft, involuntary movement, my thighs pressing together.

Laurent chuckles, dark and knowing. 'Ah, mon trésor…' his fingers trace the small of my back. 'So eager. So sweet.'

He leans down, his breath hot against my nape. 'I could ruin you right here, chérie. Would you let me?'

The air between us tightens, charged, electric.

But I don't move.

And Laurent… Laurent notices.

He hums, a pleased, wicked sound, and his hands drift lower, his touch as confident as the man himself.

'No answer?' he teases, his fingers lingering over my thighs. 'Or maybe silence is your way of begging me to continue…'

A warning. A challenge.

I grip the crate beneath me, my breath coming uneven, my body betraying me in ways I don't even have words for.

He exhales a quiet chuckle, fingers ghosting higher. 'You like this, don't you? Bent over. Trapped. Knowing you're at my mercy.'

I do. *I do.*

The realisation is dizzying, shameful, addictive.

'Say it,' he commands.

'*Yes*,' I whisper.

His hand lifts, and a second later-
Smack.
I jolt, the sound ringing through the cargo hold, a sharp burst of heat blooming across my backside.

It isn't hard. Just enough to sting, to send a jolt through me that makes my breath shudder out of my lungs.

Laurent hums, pleased. 'That was just the beginning, chérie. But I think you know that already…'

His hands return, deliberate and slow, slipping beneath the hem of my skirt, inching it higher, baring me to the cool air.

I squeeze my eyes shut, my chest rising and falling too fast, every nerve ending on fire and the second I feel his fingers hook beneath the lace of my panties, a helpless whimper slips from my throat.

Laurent hears it.

Feels it.

Loves it.

'Mmm… you're trembling already,' he peels the lace down, a slow, torturous drag, and when I shudder beneath him, he chuckles darkly. 'Let's see how much you can take.'

And then-
Smack.
Harder this time. A measured, decadent sting that sends a bolt of something wicked straight to my core.

My knees wobble, my fingers tightening around the crate as a broken sound leaves my lips.

Laurent strokes over the heat he's left behind, fingertips tracing the burn, soft and reverent, before he murmurs-

'Count for me, Quinn.'

My heart slams against my ribs.

Oh god.

I swallow hard, my voice thin, barely a whisper. 'One.'

He makes a pleased noise, his touch featherlight as he trails his palm up my spine. 'Good girl.'

Another comes.

Smack.

I jolt, my breath stuttering, my body trembling in ways I can't contain. It stings, it burns - but worse than that is the way the heat coils low, the way my thighs press together, desperate for something I refuse to name.

'Two,' I gasp, my voice shaking.

Laurent hums in approval, his fingers dragging down the length of my thigh before teasing back up, the contrast between the harsh and the soft making me crazy.

Smack.

'*Fuck.*'

The sound is obscene, my body reacting before I can stop it, my back arching, my hips shifting toward the pressure.

I hate how much I love it.

I hate how much I need it.

My voice is broken when I whisper-

'Three.'

Laurent chuckles. 'Mmm... I think you're starting to like this, chérie.'

I bite my lip, my face flaming, my breath ragged.

Another lands.

Smack.

I moan before I can stop myself.

'*Oh god.*'

I grip the crate tighter, my body shaking, pleasure and pain tangling together in a way that makes it impossible to separate them.

'*Four*,' I whisper, barely able to hear my own voice over the rush of blood in my ears.

Laurent's other hand settles firm against the small of my back, holding me in place, keeping me right where he wants me. 'Such a perfect little thing. Falling apart for me.'

I squeeze my eyes shut, the heat too much, the tension

unbearable.

I'm slipping. Sinking.

And I want- I need-

SMACK.

The fifth is the hardest yet.

It's too much.

It's not *enough*.

I shudder, a choked sound escaping me as my head falls forward, my breath tumbling out in a desperate, gasping moan.

'*Five,*' I manage, my voice weak, wrecked.

Laurent exhales, long and slow, his hands skimming my thighs, my hips, tracing over the heat of his punishment like he's committing it to memory.

Then, finally, he leans in, his lips brushing my ear.

My breath stutters, my fingers still gripping the crate beneath me, my skin thrumming with heat, the lingering sting of his touch branding me.

And then-

Behind me, I hear it.

A slow, deliberate slide of metal teeth.

The sound of his zipper lowering.

A fresh wave of heat rushes through me, molten, dangerous, pooling low in my stomach as every nerve tightens, every muscle coils.

I don't move.

I can't move.

I just stay bent over, my skirt bunched high, my lace pooled around my thighs, my swollen pussy framed, my breath shallow and unsteady as Laurent's hands return, skimming up my hips, slow and possessive.

'Now...' his voice is velvet, teasing, laced with satisfaction. 'Let's see how well you take direction, chérie.'

A warm breath ghosts over my neck, his body closing in

behind mine, caging me in, his presence a dark, dizzying weight pressing into every inch of me.

And I realise, in this breathless, breaking moment-

I wouldn't dream of stopping him.

*

My breath catches, my pulse hammering as his hands roam my body, smoothing over the curves he's just finished punishing, worshiping me with reverent fingers.

'You're shaking,' he murmurs, voice like dark velvet. His palm spreads possessively over my backside, his fingers skimming down, teasing, learning me inch by inch. 'Is it fear, or are you just that desperate for me?'

I swallow hard. 'You already know.'

His low chuckle sends a ripple of heat through me. 'Yes, I do,' he admits, leaning in, his lips brushing the shell of my ear. 'But I want to hear you say it, chérie.'

His touch drifts lower, and I gasp as he presses against me, thick and insistent. My fingers tighten on the cargo crate, bracing, every muscle coiled, burning.

'Tell me you want this,' his voice is rough now, control slipping. 'Tell me how badly you need it.'

I squeeze my eyes shut, lips parting, but no words come at first. I'm lost to the anticipation, to the way he's drawing this out, savouring every moment and then I hear myself whisper.

Beg.

'Fuck me.'

Laurent curses, low and filthy.

And then he moves.

The first slow thrust steals the air from my lungs, a moan slipping free before I can stop it. His hands flex against my hips, grip tightening like he's holding himself back, barely.

He rocks forward again, deeper this time, and my knees

threaten to buckle.

'Merde, you feel so good…' his voice is almost guttural now, every ounce of that suave control beginning to crack. 'So tight. So perfect. I knew you would be.'

I gasp, nails scraping against the crate beneath me, but Laurent doesn't let up. He rolls his hips, slow and deliberate, pushing me to the brink with each perfect movement.

'Don't hold back,' he coaxes, voice thick with satisfaction. 'Let me hear you, Quinn. Give me every sound, every moan-' his next thrust is deeper, a sharp snap of his hips that has me crying out. 'Ah, that's it…'

His fingers slip into my hair, tilting my head back, forcing me to arch. His mouth finds my neck, lips brushing heat against my pulse.

'You're so beautiful like this…' his grip on my waist tightens, a shudder racking through him as he buries himself deeper. 'Mine, for this moment. Do you feel it?'

I do.

Every inch of me feels him.

He moves faster, harder now, restraint slipping, the sounds of our bodies colliding swallowed by the roar of the engines. My breath stutters, hands fisting, pleasure coiling impossibly tight inside me.

Laurent's grip on my hips tightens like he's anchoring himself, his breaths turning ragged, uneven. I can feel the tremor in his body, the way his muscles flex and strain with every thrust, his control fraying at the edges. He's usually so composed, so smooth, but now - now he's losing himself in me, and the thought makes my stomach clench with something far deeper than lust.

His hands are greedy - dragging up my spine, threading into my hair, gripping my hips like he owns me. His control is slipping, cracking open beneath the force of it, and the sound that rumbles from his throat - half curse, half groan - sends another sharp pulse of pleasure through me, his forehead pressing between my shoulder blades for half a second before he forces himself upright again, his hands sliding up my waist, spanning my ribs.

It's not enough.

I need more-

I need to touch him, to feel him, skin to skin.

Without thinking, I reach back, my fingers searching, and he catches them instantly, his palm covering mine, pressing my hand against the rough muscle of his thigh. A shiver rolls through him at the contact, and then he's lacing our fingers together, squeezing tight, grounding himself in me.

I squeeze my eyes shut, teeth sinking into my lip to stop the noise threatening to spill out.

A moan escapes me, not just from the pleasure, but from the intimacy of it - this unexpected tenderness, this moment of connection in the midst of something so raw, so primal.

'Quinn,' he groans, my name unraveling from his lips like a prayer, like a plea. His thrusts grow erratic, desperate, every movement a barely contained tremor of need.

I shake my head, biting harder, but he's not having it.

A rough hand slides up, curling around my throat - not tight, just there, just enough to make my pulse skitter. He leans in, his lips brushing my ear. 'I want to hear you. Now.'

A sound breaks from me, sharp and unbidden, my body trembling at his command.

'That's it,' he rasps, his movements turning erratic, desperate. 'Let me feel it.'

I can't stop it.

I can't hold it back.

Pleasure crashes through me like a rogue wave, knocking the breath from my lungs. My body clenches around him, my vision going white-hot as I fall, as I break, as I shudder through the most devastating release of my life.

Laurent curses, his grip tightening, his rhythm faltering as he feels it, as he's pulled under with me. His fingers slide down, dig in, his whole body shuddering against mine. His hands are everywhere - gripping my hips, sliding up my sides, skimming the curve of my ribs as if he needs to feel every inch of me. His control is slipping, his composure cracking open like glass under pressure, and the realization makes my pulse hammer even harder.

'Fuck, Quinn-'

I bite my lip, trying to stay quiet, but the pressure is unbearable. '*Mr Laurent-*'

He groans at the sound of his name, his hand smoothing up my spine, fingers tangling in my hair as he pulls my head back just enough to bring his lips to my ear. 'Louder.'

His voice is pure command, roughened by need, by want, by something deeper than either of us can name. I shake my head, eyes squeezed shut, because I can't - because if I let go, if I give in completely, I'll be lost.

'Come with me,' he rasps, his lips at my shoulder, his teeth grazing, his body shuddering as he pushes deeper. 'Let go, let me *feel* you-'

His groan is wrecked, his body locking up as he thrusts deep, his breath hot against my shoulder.

Then he's gone, lost, breaking apart with a sharp, guttural growl as he spills into me, as his body jerks, as he shudders through his own ruin.

And it hits me like a tsunami, like freefall, like the moment before impact when there's nothing but sensation.

A cry rips from my throat, my whole body seizing around him, shaking apart, and Laurent follows with a broken groan, his grip on my hand turning vice-like as he presses deep, every muscle in his body going taut.

For a moment, there's nothing but breath, the thundering of our heartbeats, the lingering echoes of our release in the thick, pressurised air.

Neither of us moves, neither of us speaks.

He slumps forward, his forehead pressing between my shoulder blades, his chest rising and falling against my back. He's still holding my hand, still tangled with me like he can't quite bring himself to let go.

Then, slowly, he drags in a breath, his lips ghosting across my bare shoulder.

'Mon dieu,' he exhales, his voice raw, spent. 'I think I may have just died and gone to heaven.'

*

CHAPTER FIVE

I stand there for a long moment, my hands braced against the cool metal, my breath still uneven, my body still trembling with the aftershocks of what just happened.

Of what I just let happen.

Laurent is gone, his presence retreating up the access steps, leaving only the ghost of his touch lingering over my skin, the imprint of his hands still hot on my thighs, my hips, my spine.

I exhale shakily, my pulse hammering as I slowly straighten, feeling the sharp sting where he left his mark. My behind throbs in time with my heartbeat, a pulsing ache laced with pleasure.

I shouldn't like it.

I shouldn't crave it.

And yet, I bite my lip as the sensation hums through me, deep and molten, curling low in my belly.

With a trembling hand, I smooth my skirt back down over

my thighs, wincing at the way the fabric drags over my sensitised skin. My lace is still bunched high, tangled in the aftermath, and I force myself to fix it, to pull it back into place even as my body protests. Even as the illicit warmth between my legs reminds me exactly what I just did.

I press a palm to my chest, willing my heart to slow. Willing my mind to catch up.

I redress carefully, methodically, pulling myself back together piece by piece. Tugging my blouse into place, straightening my tie, smoothing my hair. My fingers still shake as I check my reflection in the gleaming surface of a metal crate, catching the flush still high on my cheeks, the slight part of my lips, the wildness still lingering in my eyes.

I inhale deeply, trying to steady myself, trying to regain the composure I know I'll need when I step back into that cabin.

I've never done this before. Never crossed this line. Never let myself go like that.

And yet... I'm tingling with the thrill of it. Still pulsing with it.

I swallow hard, pressing my thighs together, forcing my expression into something neutral, something professional. I have a job to do.

I lift my chin, exhaling slowly, and make my way toward the ladder.

Time to go back.

Time to face them.

Again.

My fingers curl around the bottle Laurent left for me, the glass cool against my heated skin. It's heavier than I expect, thick and decadent, something expensive, indulgent - like everything about him. I hold it close, cradling it against my chest as I walk toward the steps, my pulse still erratic, my body still thrumming.

I take a breath, willing myself steady, willing my legs to

stop trembling as I ascend, one slow foot at a time. My uniform feels too tight now, my blouse clinging to my skin, my skirt shifting against the places where Laurent's hands lingered, branding me.

And yet, even as my body still hums with the imprint of him, my thoughts shift.

Hale.

He'll be up there now, back in his seat, back with the others.

Waiting.

Watching.

My stomach clenches, my breath quickening as I imagine his gaze locking onto me the moment I step through the panel, the sharp cut of his stare raking over me, seeing too much, knowing too much.

Because Hale isn't like the others.

Laurent is indulgence, Carter is charm - but Hale? Hale is something else entirely.

Darker.

He doesn't flirt, he doesn't tease.

He watches.

He waits.

And I have no doubt he'll see everything.

I swallow hard, adjusting my grip on the bottle as I reach the top of the steps, pressing a steadying hand to the frame. One more breath, one more second to compose myself - then I push open the panel and step back into the cabin, my heart hammering as I brace myself for what comes next.

Then, finally, I emerge back into the cabin.

The lighting is softer here, the hum of the engines smoother. Laurent is reclined, his glass of champagne in hand, completely at ease. Carter is sprawled out, his expression unreadable but amused, fingers tapping idly against his knee.

And Hale-

Hale is watching me.

Not casually. Not playfully.

Watching.

His dark gaze pins me as I step forward, quiet, steady, assessing. He says nothing, but it's the silence that unsettles me the most. Because it means he sees me. Really sees me.

My fingers tighten around the bottle, pressing it to my chest as I force my feet to keep moving.

Not over.

Not by a long shot.

I move through the cabin with measured steps, bottle cradled carefully in my hands. The weight of their eyes settles over me, but I keep my chin high, my expression schooled into something smooth, controlled.

Laurent grins as I set the bottle down on the glossy wood of the table between them, his gaze flicking from it to me with unguarded excitement.

'Ah, magnifique,' he murmurs, fingers tracing the label in appreciation. 'You've no idea how difficult this was to acquire.'

I reach for the cork, twisting carefully. 'The pressure in the cabin means the carbonation will dissipate faster than it would on the ground,' I explain, keeping my voice even. 'We should drink quickly if you want to enjoy it at its best.'

Laurent gives a low, indulgent hum. 'A shame to rush something so exquisite... but I suppose we must.'

The cork eases free with a soft pop, not the celebratory burst it would have on the ground, but a more muted release. The rich, golden liquid fizzes up briefly as I tilt the bottle, then settles almost immediately as I pour.

I pass the first glass to Carter, who takes his time, his fingers brushing against mine as he accepts it. Just a whisper of contact, deliberate and unhurried, a silent acknowledgment that tightens something low in my stomach.

Laurent is just as bold, his thumb dragging deliberately over my skin as he takes his own, smirking at the way my breath catches.

And then there's Hale.

I turn to him, offering the final glass. He doesn't reach for it right away, just looks at me, his gaze unreadable, sharp.

Then, finally, he takes it.

No contact. No lingering touch. Just cool fingers wrapping around the glass and pulling it away.

Rejection? Restraint?

I can't tell. But the absence of it lingers more than the others' touch combined.

*

I take a slow breath, pressing my hands against the cool counter in the galley. The engines hum, steady and constant, but inside me, everything is unsteady. My body still thrums, my skin still tingles, my mind still spins with the heat of it all.

I reach for a glass of water, taking a slow sip, trying to pull myself back together. *You're fine. Just breathe.*

A shift in the air makes me pause. Then, footsteps.

I already know who it is before I turn.

Hale leans against the doorway, arms crossed, gaze dark and unreadable. He doesn't speak right away, just watches me like he's weighing something up.

'You alright?' he asks at last, voice low, even.

I blink, forcing my expression into something neutral. 'Of course. Why wouldn't I be?'

His eyes flicker over me, taking in every detail. The slight flush still on my skin, the way I'm gripping the counter like I need the grounding.

'No reason,' he says, but there's something behind it. A

weight.

He shifts forward just slightly, close enough that I catch the faint scent of his cologne - something darker than Laurent's, something that lingers like smoke.

'They can be a lot,' he adds, voice quieter now. 'I know that.'

I swallow, my fingers flexing against the counter. He's not asking me what happened. He's not prying. Just watching, just knowing.

'You didn't have to check on me,' I murmur.

Hale tilts his head, considering. 'Didn't have to. Wanted to.'

That shouldn't make my stomach flip. But it does.

A beat of silence passes between us, thick with something unspoken. He shifts like he's about to step back, to turn away, and I know if I let him go now, he won't push.

He's not like Laurent, not like Carter.

He won't chase me down.

But something in me won't let him leave.

Before I can think too hard about it, my fingers reach out, brushing lightly against his wrist. It's barely a touch, barely anything at all, but it stops him like I've yanked him back.

His gaze flicks to where my hand lingers, then back to me, eyes sharp, questioning.

'Wait,' I breathe, softer than I mean to.

He doesn't move, doesn't speak, his patience a stark contrast to the heat curling low in my stomach.

I lick my lips, my pulse unsteady. 'You-' I hesitate, searching for the right words. *You make me nervous. You make me curious. You make me want things I shouldn't.*

What comes out instead is, 'What do you think of me?'

His brows draw together, just slightly. 'What kind of question is that?'

I shrug, trying to act like it's casual, like my skin isn't

burning from the inside out. 'An honest one.'

Hale watches me for a long moment, and then, slowly, he steps closer. The space between us shrinks, the air thickens, my breath catches.

'You want honesty?' he murmurs, voice low, rough around the edges. His gaze flickers over me, slow, intense, lingering.

I swallow hard, nodding.

He leans in, close enough that his breath grazes my cheek.

'I think you're dangerous,' he says, his voice a rasp, dark and deliberate.

My pulse jumps. 'Me?'

'Yeah,' he murmurs, his fingers skimming just barely along my forearm, a touch so light it makes me shiver. 'Because you make me want to break my own rules.'

The words hit me deep, deeper than I expect, leaving me breathless, weightless.

Hale holds my gaze for a fraction longer, something raw flickering behind his restraint. Then, with a slow, deliberate movement, he eases back, like he's giving me the choice.

To stop him.

To let him go.

To cross the line completely.

And I don't know which one I want more.

I grip his wrist, pulling him toward me before I can second-guess it. The motion is instinctive, desperate, but the second he's there, right in front of me, I freeze.

I can't breathe.

The space between us crackles, charged, unbearable. Our eyes lock, and I swear the entire plane ceases to exist, narrowing down to just him, just us.

He doesn't move at first. He just watches me, his dark eyes unreadable, assessing. I feel the heat of him, the sheer presence of him, and my heart hammers so hard I think he might hear it.

Then, slowly, he reaches in, his fingers trailing up my hip, deliberate, exploring. I shudder beneath his touch, heat licking up my spine. He waits, gauging my reaction, giving me a chance to pull away.

I don't.

His grip tightens, just slightly, and then-

We collide.

It's not soft, not hesitant. It's a breaking point, an inevitability. My hands fist in his shirt, dragging him closer as his lips crash against mine. It's fierce, hot, a kiss that steals the breath from my lungs.

He groans low in his throat, one hand gripping my waist, the other threading into my hair, angling me to take him deeper. I melt, surrendering, pressing up into him as he presses down, until there's no space, no hesitation, just heat, just hunger.

I don't know which one of us is shaking harder.

He deepens the kiss, his grip possessive, like he's been holding back for too long and now he can't - won't - stop. His fingers tighten in my hair, tugging just enough to send a shiver down my spine, my lips parting on a gasp that he swallows greedily.

His other hand roams, sliding down my waist, gripping my hip, pulling me flush against him. There's no mistaking how hard he is, how much he wants this. A growl rumbles in his chest as he presses me back against the narrow counter, caging me in with the sheer force of him.

I'm drowning, burning.

My hands skate over his chest, desperate to feel him, to memorize every ridge of muscle beneath his crisp shirt. His breath is heavy, hot against my lips as he moves lower, his mouth tracing a searing path along my jaw, down the column of my throat.

'Quinn,' he murmurs, the sound rough, like it's been

ripped from somewhere deep inside him. His lips graze my pulse point, his teeth dragging lightly, sending a jolt straight through me.

I gasp, head tilting back, surrendering to his touch. His hand is already beneath my blouse, fingers splaying against my heated skin, the contrast of his calloused palm and my softness making me tremble.

'Hale...' my voice is barely a whisper, but he hears it, responds to it, his hand sliding higher, his thumb brushing over the edge of my lace. My stomach clenches, anticipation coiling tight.

He exhales hard, his forehead pressing against mine for a beat, as if he's fighting for control, battling something between desire and restraint.

'Tell me to stop,' he rasps.

I shake my head, my fingers clutching at his shirt, pulling him closer. 'Don't you dare.'

*

A dark sound rumbles from his chest, approval, possession. Then his mouth is on mine again, fiercer this time, more desperate. His hands roam freely now, gripping, exploring, learning every inch of me.

I arch into him, craving more, aching for it. His thigh nudges between mine, pressing just right, sending a sharp pulse of pleasure rocketing through me.

I whimper, and it undoes him.

He groans against my lips, his hands gripping my hips, lifting me onto the narrow counter like I weigh nothing. His fingers slide up my thighs, pushing my skirt higher, his touch rough, urgent.

'I shouldn't be doing this,' he breathes, his lips trailing down my throat, across my collarbone, igniting every nerve in my body.

'Then stop,' I challenge, voice trembling.

His eyes flick up, dark, molten. 'You know I won't.'

And then he's kissing me again, his hands greedy, his body pressing me into the counter as the heat between us threatens to consume us whole.

My fingers tremble as I work at his belt, the button, the zipper - desperate, frantic, lost in the need clawing through me. The moment I free him, he lets out a rough, strangled groan, his forehead pressing against mine, his breath heavy and uneven.

He twitches in my grasp, thick and heated in my palm, and I swear I feel him shudder as I stroke him, feeling every inch of his smooth, rigid length. My breath catches.

God, he's big.

Heavy.

Perfect.

He exhales sharply, his hands gripping my thighs, parting them wider, making space for himself between them.

'Fuck, Quinn...'

His voice is hoarse, barely more than a growl, and then his fingers slide over mine, guiding my touch, making me feel just how badly he needs this - needs me.

I can't breathe.

I can't think.

I only know the way my own body pulses with want, the way my thighs tighten around him, the way I ache for him to take me, to shatter me completely.

'You have no idea what you do to me,' he mutters, his lips brushing against my jaw, my cheek, his breath scorching against my skin. He's barely holding it together - I can hear it in his voice, feel it in the way his fingers flex against my hips, like he's on the verge of losing himself.

I swallow hard, my own restraint hanging by a thread.

'Then stop holding back,' I whisper.

His breath hitches, and then his grip tightens. One hand slides higher, fingertips tracing the edge of my panties, pushing the thin fabric aside - baring me to him completely.

A sharp gasp catches in my throat as he touches me, teasing, testing. My body jerks, heat flooding through me, and he groans when he feels it, feels how soaked I am for him.

'Jesus, Quinn...' His forehead presses against mine again, like he's trying to steady himself, but he's already slipping, already unraveling.

I part my thighs more, silent permission, silent pleading.

And then I feel him, thick and hot, nudging against my entrance, pressing inside, stretching me inch by inch, sinking deep, so deep I can't stop the sharp, keening cry that escapes my lips.

Hale exhales a ragged breath, his fingers digging into my hips as he holds me still, buried inside me. 'You feel...' his voice catches, strained and rough. 'So fucking perfect.'

I'm trembling, gasping, trying to breathe, trying to hold onto something solid, but all I have is him - his hands gripping me, his body pressing me against the galley wall, his heat fusing with mine.

Then he moves.

Slow, at first.

Measured.

Controlled.

I tighten around him, hips tilting to take him deeper, and he loses it.

His grip turns bruising, his rhythm hard and deep, sending pleasure crashing through me with every thrust. My head falls back, nails raking across his back, my body arching as he drives into me, relentless, unstoppable.

His lips crush against mine, swallowing my moans,

claiming me completely. He's everywhere-inside me, around me, drowning me in sensation, in pleasure so intense I can barely stand it.

'*Hale...*' his name tumbles from my lips, raw and desperate, and something about it unravels him further.

'Come for me, Quinn,' he rasps, voice rough, raw - desperate. 'I need to feel you.'

His words detonate inside me, pushing me past the point of no return. My body locks up, spine arching, mouth falling open as pleasure slams through me, tearing me apart.

'Oh, god-' the cry spills from my lips, unrestrained, lost beneath the roar of the engines, swallowed by the heat of him, the weight of him, the way he drives into me, dragging me through the shuddering aftershocks of my release.

My fingers claw at his back, digging in as I convulse around him, pulsing, squeezing, every part of me tightening, gripping.

I feel everything - every slick, desperate thrust, every ounce of his control fracturing, his body chasing oblivion.

And then he's gone.

A choked curse rumbles from deep in his throat, his rhythm breaking, faltering, his whole body shuddering. His grip turns bruising on my hips, his fingers pressing hard enough to leave their mark as he buries himself deep, shaking apart, coming inside me.

The heat of it, the rawness of it, steals the air from my lungs.

I feel him, thick and hot, mixing with the remnants of Laurent - the memory of Carter still lingering on my skin. The sheer filth of it sends a fresh tremor through me, my body still rippling, still clenching around him as he pulses, emptying himself, filling me up until I'm dripping.

His head drops to mine, forehead pressing against my temple, his breath ragged, his body trembling with the aftershocks of his own release.

For a long moment, we stay like that, our bodies locked together, fused by sweat and something far more dangerous. His heart hammers against mine, erratic and wild, our breaths tangled, uneven.

His fingers skim down my side, a lazy, reverent touch, and then his lips brush mine - just once, barely a whisper of contact - but it's enough to send another shiver through me, another aftershock of sensation, as if my body is still trying to process everything I've just done.

I don't move.

I can't.

My limbs feel liquid, my pulse an unsteady staccato in my throat.

Hale shifts, exhaling against my cheek, his hands still tracing absent patterns over my skin. 'Are you okay?'

I breathe in deeply, letting my eyes flutter shut for a second, absorbing the way his voice sounds now - deeper, rougher, edged with something softer, something... almost tender.

I don't know what this is.

I don't know what I've just done.

But as I slowly open my eyes and meet his, still dark, still burning...

I drop.

My knees meet the cool floor of the galley, my body still thrumming, trembling, as I slide down the length of him, as my fingers curl around his thighs, keeping him steady. His breath catches, sharp, his muscles going rigid, but he doesn't stop me. He doesn't move at all - just watches, silent and dangerous, as I tilt my head back and meet his gaze, his spent length still heavy, still glistening, his release slick between my thighs.

I don't think. I just act.

My tongue flicks out, catching the taste of him first - salt and sin and something utterly intoxicating. He jerks, his entire body tensing, his fingers clenching into fists at his sides as I part my lips and take him inside, warm, wet, soft.

A deep, guttural sound rumbles from his chest, raw and unguarded. 'Quinn-'

I hum, feeling him twitch against my tongue, my own satisfaction pooling low in my belly as I take more, deeper, hollowing my cheeks, savouring every inch, every shudder that racks through him.

His hand finds my hair, fingers tangling at the base of my skull - not pulling, not guiding, just gripping. Holding. As if I'm the only thing keeping him grounded, keeping him from losing whatever shred of control he has left.

But it's slipping. I can feel it.

He's still so sensitive, still on edge, his body betraying him with the way his hips twitch forward, the way his breath shudders out of him, the way his thighs tremble under my touch.

'Fuck-'

It's barely a breath, barely a whisper, but it coils through me, setting my skin alight, making me desperate for more.

I take my time. I savour him. Every inch. Every taste. I let my tongue drag, slow and deliberate, feeling him throb, feeling him tense, feeling him come undone for me, because of me.

His head tips back against the wall, a low growl escaping through gritted teeth, his chest heaving. His hand tightens in my hair, still not guiding, just holding on as I worship him, as I take him deeper, as I refuse to waste a single drop of his gift.

His thighs flex, his abs tighten, his breath turns ragged - he's so close, so near the edge again, and I don't stop, don't let up, don't give him a second to recover.

And then- he breaks.

His hand wrenches at my hair, his body jerking as he pulses against my tongue, spilling himself once more. I take it all, every last drop, swallowing him down, feeling him shake beneath my touch, feeling the raw, unfiltered intensity of him coming apart for me.

He groans, deep and low, a sound that makes my core clench, that sends another wave of heat crashing through me.

I stay there, kneeling before him, my hands still gripping his thighs, my lips still parted as I slowly, deliberately, lick the last traces of him from my mouth.

When I finally look up, his eyes are on me.

Dark. Hungry. Ravaged.

And then-

He yanks me up, his mouth crashing onto mine, his kiss bruising, possessive, as if he can still taste himself on my lips. As if he needs to claim me all over again.

Then he steps back, his dark eyes raking over me - taking in the sight of my swollen lips, my flushed cheeks, my tousled hair, my ruined uniform, the way my chest still rises and falls in uneven waves, my body still pulsing, still craving, still hungry for more.

I bite down, tasting the remnants of him, heat coiling low in my belly, my legs trembling beneath me.

He watches me for a beat longer, something unreadable flickering behind his gaze - something raw, something dangerous. Then, with a sharp inhale, he blinks.

Nods.

Wordlessly, he reaches down, buckling himself back into place, his fingers moving deftly, his shoulders tense. Another breath, short and sharp, before he steps back, putting distance between us, though the space is still thick with something neither of us name.

And then - he turns.

Without another word, without another look, and he

strides for the exit, disappearing back into the cabin, leaving me breathless, shaking, alone.

*

I half-gasp as tremor rolls through me. I press my back against the cool galley counter, my legs trembling, my breath unsteady. My pulse is a hammer against my ribs, my skin flushed and slick, every nerve ending still buzzing, still alight with the echoes of their hands, their mouths, their bodies.

I can still feel them.

All of them.

Carter's rough grip, his hungry need, the way he pushed me over the edge with a wicked smile. Laurent's teasing dominance, his slow, deliberate torment, the way he owned my body like it had always belonged to him. And Hale... dark, brooding Hale, the one who broke the rules right alongside me, who came undone with me, who wanted me in a way that felt almost *dangerous*.

I should feel ashamed.

I should feel mortified.

I should feel *something* other than this wild, hot ache still throbbing inside me.

But all I feel is satisfaction.

A deep, dark satisfaction that scares me.

I close my eyes, swallowing against the lump in my throat, my thoughts unraveling, slipping between memories like a dirty film reel looping in my head.

I've never done this before.

Never once crossed the line with a passenger, never allowed myself to be anything other than perfectly controlled, perfectly poised.

My body is my own, my choices always dictated by restraint, by discipline.

And yet, I've surrendered to them. Not just one of them. All of them.

What does that make me?

The thought crashes into me, hot and sharp, and I press my palms against the counter, trying to steady myself.

I should feel dirty. I should feel used. But I don't.

I feel *powerful*.

I *let* them take me. I *let* them. I *chose* this. I *wanted* it.

A slow shiver rolls through me as the realization takes root, spreading deep, curling warm and possessive around my core.

This wasn't them taking advantage of me. This wasn't them using me.

I was never out of control.

Not once.

And that knowledge is exhilarating.

I think back to every moment, every whispered word, every lingering touch. They were the ones who needed me. They were the ones who lost control. I was the one who let them in, who opened myself to them, who gave them the permission they didn't even realise they were seeking.

The thought makes my pulse spike, makes my thighs clench, makes my breath hitch as I stare into the dim, empty galley, my reflection faint in the stainless steel of the cabinets.

Who is this woman?

Not the perfect, poised flight attendant. Not the rule-follower.

Someone else entirely.

Someone who doesn't say no to what she wants.

Someone who doesn't hold back.

Someone who isn't afraid to let go.

And now... *now*, there's only one thing left to do.

A slow, wicked smile tugs at my lips, my pulse thrumming with dark anticipation, with *need*. It unfurls inside me, dark and thrilling, curling through my veins like liquid fire.

I let them take me.

I let them.

And I want *more*.

More than just Carter's wild hunger, more than Laurent's delicious torment, more than Hale's quiet, devastating control.

I want all of them.

Together.

I want their hands, their mouths, their bodies - all at once.

The image flashes through my mind, searing hot, dizzying in its intensity.

Laurent above me, holding me firm, owning me the way he loves to, the way he whispers I should be taken. His hands gripping my head, his voice low and taunting as he fills me, stretching me, claiming my mouth like it belongs to him.

Carter at my front, lifting me, wrecking me with those sharp, possessive thrusts, his lips bruising mine, his fingers tangled in my hair as he whispers how good I feel, how perfectly I take him.

And Hale.

Hale.

Behind me, his hand curled around my hips, guiding me, coaxing me open, his control slipping as I take all of him into me, hollowing me, stretching me as he groans, breaching me as his restraint finally shatters.

I want to be *filled*.

I want them deep inside of me, stretching me, overwhelming me, reducing me to pure pleasure. I want to feel them everywhere, want them to take me until I forget where I end and they begin.

I want to be *used*.

The thought pulses through me like a heartbeat, an ache so deep it steals my breath, makes my thighs clench, my core throb.

And I can have it.

If I just ask.

A slow, wicked smile curves my lips, my chest rising and falling with the weight of my own revelation.

I want it all.

I want them all.

And I'm done pretending otherwise.

*

CHAPTER SIX

The cabin hums with the steady thrum of the engines, the sky beyond the windows a vast expanse of black, stars winking through the darkness. The air is thick with something unspoken, something electric, something inevitable.

I step forward.

Slowly.

Deliberately.

Carter sees me first, his golden gaze flickering over me like he already knows. He leans back slightly, one arm draped over the armrest, the other resting against his thigh, his fingers tapping idly - waiting.

Not asking, not demanding.

Just waiting.

Laurent, lounging in his seat, catches my movement next. His head tilts, curiosity dancing in his dark eyes, but that wicked little smirk is already forming at the corner of his mouth, like he's been expecting this, like he planned for it.

And Hale.

Hale sits in shadow, his posture relaxed but too still, his jaw tight, his fingers flexing against his knee. He doesn't move, doesn't speak, but his eyes burn through me, assessing, searching.

Daring.

My breath is shallow, my pulse an erratic drum against my ribs.

This is it.

The final step.

I don't say a word.

Instead, I move.

I reach for Carter first, my fingers curling lightly around his wrist. His skin is warm beneath my touch, his pulse steady, strong. For a beat, he doesn't react, his eyes locked onto mine, watching, reading me, and then, ever so slowly, his lips part, a breath escaping - but still, no words.

He knows.

I give the slightest tug.

A silent command.

Come.

Then Laurent.

His smirk deepens, slow and knowing, his gaze dipping briefly over me before he exhales, as if savouring this moment. His fingers brush mine as I reach for him, deliberate and teasing, as though testing just how badly I want this.

I squeeze lightly, firm, refusing to be toyed with, and something flickers in his eyes. His smirk turns sharper, but he follows.

Come.

And then Hale.

I hesitate - just for a fraction of a second.

Not because I doubt, not because I don't want this, but because he is different. The way he looks at me, the way he holds himself, like he's fighting something within himself - like he's trying to resist.

I can't let him.

I step closer, pressing my palm against his.

His fingers twitch beneath mine.

I feel the tension in him, the coil of restraint, the controlled breathing, the slow and deliberate calm.

But he doesn't pull away.

I give him the same silent invitation, the same unspoken request.

Come.

A muscle in his jaw ticks.

A long, charged pause.

Then, finally, he moves.

One by one, they rise, the scrape of chair legs against the carpet the only sound in the cabin.

I don't look back.

I don't have to.

I feel them behind me, their presence looming, their body heat pressing in, surrounding me.

My legs feel unsteady, my breath thin, but I keep walking.

Past the flickering cabin lights.

Past the plush seats and the dim overhead glow.

Past the untouched crystal glasses, the remnants of our night scattered across the luxury that now feels inconsequential.

I lead them through the silence.

Through the dark.

Through the unspoken promises that crackle between us, alive, waiting.

The door to Carter's private sleeping quarters looms ahead.

I reach for the handle, my fingers wrapping around the cool metal.

My breath hitches.
One final moment.
One last chance to turn back.
I don't.
I push the door open, stepping inside, swallowed whole by the shadows.
No turning back.

*

The low-level lights rise gradually, casting a warm golden glow over the private suite. The room is sleek, designed for indulgence - luxury dripping from every detail - but my focus is drawn to the bed.
Large.
Centred.
Dominant.
A slow, steady pulse thrums through my body, vibrating beneath my skin as I take a step inside. My breath is shallow, the weight of the moment pressing down on my chest, filling me, stretching tight over every nerve.
Then I turn.
And they're there.
Carter. Laurent. Hale.
Following.
Closing in.
The door shuts behind them with a soft click, sealing us in together, sealing me with them.
My pulse pounds, my lungs working harder, pulling in breath after breath as they surround me, moving slowly, deliberately, each of them taking their place - one in front, one behind, one to the side - until I'm in the centre.
Caged.

Owned.

Theirs.

Carter's fingers trail down my arm, barely there, his touch featherlight but commanding. He's the first to move, stepping in close, so close, his chest nearly pressing against mine, his eyes dark and knowing as his thumb grazes the corner of my lips.

Laurent is next, circling like a predator, coming to my side, his fingers drifting over the curve of my hip, a teasing touch, a lingering brush of ownership.

And then Hale.

Silent. Towering behind me, heat rolling off his body in thick waves, his presence a solid force against my back. He doesn't touch me, not yet, but I can feel him, sense him - his restraint, his control, his need simmering beneath the surface.

I exhale sharply, a shuddering breath that gives me away.

They feel it.

They know.

I'm trembling, my body alive, aching.

My thighs press together, the anticipation unbearable, the weight of their attention sinking into me, winding me tighter, making me burn.

I swallow hard, forcing myself to speak, my voice barely above a whisper.

'So… what now?'

Carter's lips curve, his hand sliding into my hair, gripping lightly, tilting my head back so I can't look anywhere but at him.

Laurent hums lowly at my side, his fingers playing along the hem of my dress, teasing, coaxing.

Hale remains still.

Watching.

Waiting.

And then Carter speaks, his voice dark.

Final.

'Now... we ruin you.'

Fuck, yes.

The air between us is thick with heat, heavy with the weight of what's about to happen, of what I've chosen.

My breath stutters, my fingers trembling as I reach for them, all of them, my hands moving on instinct, desperate, needy. Carter's belt, Laurent's buttons, Hale's collar - I want them bare, want them against me, want *nothing* between us.

And they want the same.

Hands - so many hands - strong, urgent, relentless.

Carter is the first to move, his fingers slipping beneath the lapel of my jacket, peeling it from my shoulders, slow, deliberate, his mouth brushing against my ear as he whispers.

'Let's see what's beneath.'

A shiver rolls through me, a gasp slipping free as Laurent takes over, pulling one sleeve down, then the other, exposing me inch by inch.

My fingers curl around his wrist, needing to hold onto something, anything, as my jacket is pushed off completely, sliding down my arms, falling to the floor in a soft rustle.

Then Hale.

His hands - big, hot, unshakable - come to my front, his fingers finding the buttons of my blouse, lingering over the top one, teasing.

'Breathe,' he murmurs, his voice low, deep, wrecking.

I do. I have to.

Because the moment he begins, the moment he pushes open the first button, his knuckles brushing over my fluttering pulse, I feel like I might crumble.

The second button goes, then the third, each one exposing more of my skin, more of my need, more of the frantic hammering inside my chest.

Carter watches my face, devouring me with his eyes, his

fingers tangling into my hair, tilting my chin up, making sure I don't look anywhere but at him as Laurent parts my blouse fully, smoothing his hands over my ribs, my stomach, my waist.

A moan rises in my throat, my body thrumming, burning, wanting.

I need to feel them, all of them, need to take from them as much as they're taking from me.

With shaking hands, I reach.

Carter's belt - I unbuckle it, tugging hard, desperate to free him.

Laurent's shirt - I rip at the buttons, sending them scattering, impatient, feral.

Hale's tie - I grasp the silk, pulling him forward, pulling him into me, needing his heat, needing his weight.

A ragged groan, a sharp inhale, a quiet curse - they're losing control, too.

'She's eager,' Laurent breathes against my neck, his lips skimming the sensitive skin, making me tremble.

'I like her like this,' Carter murmurs, his hands skimming down my arms, guiding my fingers to the waistband of his slacks.

Hale exhales hard, his fingers flexing on my waist before he finally - finally - grabs the fabric of my blouse and yanks it off completely.

I gasp, my back arching, my skin bared beneath their hungry gazes, heat crackling between us, dangerous, all-consuming.

'Beautiful,' Hale mutters, almost to himself, his thumb tracing the line of my spine as Laurent's mouth presses to my collarbone, open, hot, tasting me, teasing me.

Carter groans, palming me through my lace, my body jerking at the sensation, at the way they're everywhere.

My fingers clench, nails dragging against skin, tugging at

fabric, taking, taking, taking.

And they give.

Laurent shrugs off his shirt completely, baring sculpted muscle, golden skin, a body built to ruin.

Hale unknots his tie with one pull, shrugs off his jacket, then yanks his dress shirt over his head, exposing raw strength, brutal power.

And Carter…

Carter lets me do the work, his smirk lazy as I fumble, yanking at his belt, forcing his pants lower, brushing my fingers over hard, thick, rigid heat.

His head drops forward, his lips ghosting over my cheek, my jaw, his breath shaky.

'So eager,' he mutters, his voice wrecked.

And I am.

Because this is mine.

All of them.

For me.

My lovers.

My ruin.

The air between us is thick with heat, heavy with the weight of what's coming next. My skin tingles under their stares, my heart hammering as the last barriers between us are slowly stripped away, piece by piece, stitch by delicate stitch.

Laurent's fingers skate down my ribs, slow, deliberate, teasing, before tracing the band of my lace. A gentle tug, a soft exhale as he lifts the fabric, savouring the moment before he pulls it away. His knuckles graze the underside of my breast, his breath hot against my temple as he whispers.

'Gorgeous.'

A shiver rolls through me, sharp, visceral.

Carter follows next, dropping to his knees before me, his hands smoothing over my thighs, curling beneath the hem of my panties. His eyes flick up, dark and smoldering as his fingers slip beneath the lace, rolling them down inch by inch, his lips parting as he watches more of me come into view.

My breath catches as he peels them down completely, his knuckles brushing my calves as he lifts one foot, then the other, until I step free.

The scrap of lace disappears, discarded to the floor.

I am bare.

Exposed.

Vulnerable.

Owned by their eyes, their hands, their whispers.

And yet I have never felt more in control.

My fingers twitch, needing to even the playing field.

I turn to Hale first. He's standing so still, watching, waiting, like he could devour me at any moment. My hands reach for his waistband, unfastening his slacks with slow, methodical precision. He lets me, doesn't move, doesn't breathe as I push them down his hips, revealing black briefs stretched tight over impressive length and thick, rigid heat.

A slow exhale escapes me as my palm ghosts over him, testing, measuring.

He groans, the sound rough, barely contained.

'Keep going,' he murmurs.

I do.

I strip them all.

Laurent next - his briefs are silken, expensive, decadent, and beneath them, he is long, thick, curved, a promise of sinful pleasure.

Carter last - he's smirking as I peel his final layer away, cocky and already so hard for me, his length straight, velvety, heavy in my hand.

Three men.

Three cocks.

And all of them mine.

My hands wander, moving between them, feeling them, stroking, mapping their differences, learning what makes them tremble, groan, shudder.

Hale is thick and unyielding, the kind of size that promises to stretch, to ruin.

Laurent is sleek and curved, a perfect angle, a weapon in his own right.

Carter is smooth, pulsing, steel wrapped in silk, the heat of him branding me as he murmurs, 'Look at her. Our little stewardess likes to compare.'

I do.

I love it.

The weight of them in my hands, their breaths uneven, their control slipping, the power of knowing I can make them shatter just as they've undone me.

And I've only just begun.

*

I let my hands roam, my fingers curling around their lengths, feeling the contrast between them - Carter, thick and heavy, a perfect handful, the scent of him dark and intoxicating. Laurent, elegant and refined even in this, his hardness straining toward me as though expecting my devotion. And Hale, restrained, controlled, but I can feel the tension humming beneath his skin, the way his body twitches every time my fingers move.

I don't rush.

I want to savour this moment.

I want them to feel every second of my attention, every flick of my tongue, every deliberate caress.

I start with Carter, because he's already throbbing in my grasp, his breath ragged as I stroke him slowly. His fingers tighten in my hair as I part my lips, dragging my tongue along his length, tasting salt and heat and power. His hips twitch as I tease him, barely taking him in before pulling back, licking a long, deliberate stripe that has him cursing under his breath.

'You little tease,' he mutters, voice thick.

I hum around him in response, the vibrations making him shudder, making him tighten his grip in my hair. I take him deeper, savouring the way he fills my mouth, the way he groans low in his throat when I hollow my cheeks. But just as he starts to thrust, just as he begins to unravel, I pull back, leaving him wanting.

Laurent smirks as I turn to him next, his fingers tilting my chin, his eyes flashing as he waits for me to take him in. He watches me closely, his control unshaken even as I wrap my lips around him, teasing him with slow, measured strokes of my tongue. He groans, one hand smoothing down my cheek as if he's enjoying the spectacle, savouring the power he still thinks he holds.

'Magnifique,' he murmurs, his voice a husky rasp as I swirl my tongue around him, letting my lips glide down, taking him inch by inch.

I want to ruin that composure of his. I want to see Laurent undone. So I push him deeper, working him with slow, deliberate drags of my lips, my hands gripping his thighs as I take my time worshiping him. His jaw clenches, a bead of sweat forming at his temple, and I know I have him.

And then I release him.

His head tips back with a growl, his frustration evident, but I'm already moving, already shifting toward the one I know has been holding himself back the most.

Hale.

He's been silent, watching, his dark eyes hooded and unreadable. His body is taut, muscles locked, his control near breaking point. I reach for him, and for a moment, he hesitates - just long enough for me to see the restraint he's barely clinging to.

But when my fingers curl around him, when I stroke him, feel his weight in my palm, something cracks in his gaze.

He exhales sharply, his hand cupping the back of my head as I lean in, my tongue flicking against the tip of him, tasting, teasing. He groans - deep, guttural, a sound that makes my whole body shiver. I take him slow, savouring the way his grip tightens, the way his breath grows ragged as I work him, inch by inch.

Hale is different.

He's careful, measured, but I can feel the way his body is straining, how desperately he wants to let go. His fingers tremble in my hair as I take him deeper, as I suck him slow and steady, my hands gripping his hips, urging him to move, to lose control.

And when he does - when he finally allows himself to thrust, to take what he wants - he groans my name like a man unraveling, his control snapping as he buries himself in my mouth.

I moan around him, the sound making him shudder, making his grip turn almost punishing.

I let them all have me like this, one by one, until they're panting, breathless, undone. Until they're gripping me with a desperation that matches my own, their need raw and unfiltered.

And God, I love it.

I gasp as Carter's hands find my waist, his strength undeniable as he guides me up, pulling me to my feet in one smooth motion. His mouth crashes against mine, desperate, claiming, his tongue sweeping in deep as if he's intent on stealing the very breath from my lungs. I melt into him, hands gripping his shoulders, fingers tangling in his hair, my body pressing flush to his as I surrender to the intensity of his kiss.

But he isn't just kissing me - he's moving me, walking me back toward the bed, his touch firm but reverent. When the backs of my knees hit the edge, he slows, breaking away just enough to meet my gaze. His eyes are molten, dark with intent, but he doesn't rush. Instead, he eases me down onto the cool sheets, laying me out like something precious, something to be worshipped.

And then they surround me.

Laurent to my left, Carter to my right, and Hale at my feet - three sets of hungry eyes devouring every inch of me. The heat of their gazes alone has me trembling, anticipation coiling tight in my belly as I wait, breathless, for their touch.

Laurent moves first, fingers ghosting over my collarbone, dragging lower.

'Exquisite,' he murmurs, tracing the delicate dip between my ribs, the curve of my waist, his fingertips barely grazing my skin but still managing to set me on fire.

Carter follows, his knuckles brushing the side of my throat, trailing down to my pulse, pressing just enough to feel the rapid beat beneath his touch. His thumb skims my lips, teasing, testing, before he drags his palm down my sternum, his fingers spreading wide as he explores every inch of my skin.

Hale watches, silent, unreadable, his presence an anchor to my spiraling desire. And then, finally, he moves. His hands slide up my calves, slow and methodical, kneading gently as he spreads them apart just enough to claim more space between them.

My breath catches as he strokes higher, fingertips tracing lazy circles over my inner thighs, stopping just short of where I need him most.

I whimper, shifting, chasing their hands, but they don't give me what I want. Instead, they tease.

They linger.

Laurent's lips brush my ear, his breath hot and shivery as he whispers something filthy in French, his hands skimming my ribs, teasing the undersides of my breasts but never quite touching. Carter's mouth follows suit, tracing the line of my jaw, down my throat, his teeth grazing, his tongue soothing, never lingering long enough to satisfy.

And Hale - God, Hale - his hands are fire and ice, stroking, squeezing, spreading my thighs wider only to retreat, his thumbs brushing just close enough to make me ache, his control maddening.

I writhe beneath them, my body a live wire of sensation, every nerve ending singing, begging. I don't know whose touch I need more, who I want to break me first. My fingers claw at the sheets, my breath coming in short, stuttering gasps as I tip my head back, surrendering to the slow, torturous build.

Laurent chuckles, a low, wicked sound. 'Patience, chérie,' he murmurs, his lips grazing my temple, his fingers continuing their lazy exploration. 'We have all night.'

The promise in his voice sends a violent shudder through me.

All night.

I don't know if I'll survive it.

Laurent's fingers trace up my throat, his touch excruciating. He lingers at my chin, tilting my face to meet his gaze, his pupils blown wide with hunger. His lips part as if to speak, but then he doesn't - he just watches me, waiting. The anticipation is unbearable, my pulse hammering in my throat. I don't want him to wait. I don't want any of them to wait. I want to feel all of them.

I reach for him first, letting my fingers curl around his length, feeling the weight of him, the heat, the throb that matches my own pulse. His groan is low, guttural, slipping through his clenched teeth as I stroke him slowly, deliberately.

I love how he responds to me, how his breath stutters, how his fingers tighten against my jaw, a silent plea for more.

And then Carter is at my side, his own breath hot against my ear as his hands map my skin. He slides down my body, his fingers gliding over my ribs, my stomach, teasing lower, exploring, learning.

My back arches off the sheets, desperate for more contact, but it's Hale who gives it to me - his touch firm, knowing, his hands bracketing my hips as he settles between my thighs. My breath catches, a sharp inhale as he strokes me open, as his fingers slide through the glistening evidence of how much I want this.

'So ready for us,' he murmurs, his voice gravel and smoke, heavy with restraint.

Laurent finally claims my mouth then, no longer waiting, his kiss deep, demanding, his tongue sweeping over mine in slow, indulgent strokes. I moan against him, a sound that turns to a gasp as Hale works me, teasing me apart, drawing me higher, his fingers moving in steady, devastating precision

Carter moves then, shifting closer, taking my hand and guiding it to him. I wrap my fingers around him, feeling the contrast - he's heavier, thicker, the heat of him searing against my palm. I stroke him in time with Laurent, loving the way their bodies respond to me, the way their breaths syncopate, growing heavier, rougher.

And then Hale presses deeper, curling his fingers just right, and my hips jerk against his hand, pleasure crackling through me in an electric pulse.

'I can feel you,' he murmurs, his lips brushing the inside of my thigh. 'Let go.'

I whimper into Laurent's kiss, my body trembling,

overwhelmed, unraveling. There's nowhere to run from it, no escape from the pleasure they're giving me, and I don't want to run. I want to drown in it. I want to surrender completely.

Carter's hand cups my breast, his thumb brushing over my hardened peak, while Laurent's kiss grows hungrier, his fingers threading through my hair, anchoring me to him. And beneath it all, Hale pushes me higher, deeper, until my body is nothing but sensation, nothing but need.

'Let go, Quinn,' Laurent breathes against my lips, and I do.

I *shatter*.

Pleasure rips through me, a tidal wave I can't contain, my body convulsing, my breath breaking, my moans muffled against Laurent's mouth as Hale doesn't stop, doesn't let up, pushing me through it, making it last. My grip tightens on Carter, my body shaking between them, consumed, utterly lost.

And when it finally ebbs, when the aftershocks leave me trembling and gasping, they don't move away. They stay close, surrounding me, their touches reverent, grounding me, making sure I don't slip too far away.

Hale presses a lingering kiss to my thigh. Carter strokes my hair. Laurent watches me with something unreadable in his eyes, his thumb brushing my lips, as if memorising me like this - ruined, undone, and entirely theirs.

And I am.

I am.

Carter shifts beneath me, his hands guiding my thighs as I straddle him, his skin fever-hot against mine. My palms press against his chest, feeling the steady, powerful thrum of his heartbeat beneath my fingertips. It's strong, grounding, and for a moment, I just stay there, poised above him, my breath coming in slow, shaking waves.

Laurent's hands find my hips, his grip firm, steadying me as I hover, as if he knows I need a moment to take this in - to take them all in. His lips brush the back of my shoulder, a whisper of heat against my skin, his breath warm, reverent. 'Take your time, chérie.'

Hale strokes a hand down my spine, his touch so light it sends shivers cascading down my body, heightening every nerve ending, making me hyperaware of them all around me. His fingers trace the dip of my back, soothing, coaxing, worshipping. 'We've got you,' he murmurs, his voice lower now, rougher. 'Just let go.'

I exhale slowly, sinking down, and the moment Carter fills me, a sigh spills from my lips, pleasure unfurling like silk through my limbs. He groans beneath me, his hands flexing on my thighs, his muscles tightening. 'Jesus, Quinn...'

My head tilts back, a shuddering gasp slipping free as Laurent presses closer, his hands guiding my hips in a slow, steady rhythm, making me feel every inch of Carter as I move. There's no rush, no urgency - just this slow, indulgent rhythm, like they want to make this last forever.

'Look at her,' Laurent murmurs, his voice thick with admiration, his hands gliding up my sides, tracing my curves like he's memorising every inch. 'She's perfect.'

Hale makes a sound behind me, something between agreement and awe, and then his lips are at the nape of my neck, pressing soft, open-mouthed kisses against my skin. His hand slides up, threading through my hair, tipping my head slightly, giving him better access as his mouth moves lower, as his breath skates over my heated skin.

Carter's hands move, one smoothing up my stomach, fingertips ghosting over my ribs, teasing the sensitive place just beneath my breasts. The other drifts lower, gripping my thigh, holding me against him as I move, as I melt into the sensation, as their hands and mouths send wave after wave of pleasure through me.

I feel worshipped.

Cherished.
Utterly adored.
Every touch is reverent, every glance heavy with meaning. It's not just raw need - not just hunger or lust.
It's more.
It's them wanting me.
All of me.
Laurent's hand glides down, slipping between us, adding another layer of sensation, and I cry out, my body clenching, pleasure hitting me in sharp, liquid waves. I can feel Carter tense beneath me, his grip tightening, his breath turning ragged.
'That's it,' he rasps. 'Take what you need.'
I sink deeper, roll my hips just right, and the pleasure rises again, consuming me, overwhelming me. My hands tighten against Carter's chest, nails biting into his skin as I chase it, as I let myself be taken by it.
Hale's lips move to my shoulder, his breath a soft, shuddering thing against my skin. 'You feel incredible,' he murmurs. 'So beautiful like this.'
Laurent's fingers move faster, his breath hitching against my ear as he watches me fall apart. 'Let go, Quinn.'
And I do.
The pleasure crashes over me. shattering me all over again, and I'm not alone in it. They hold me through it - Carter gripping my hips as he groans my name, Laurent pressing his body against mine, steadying me, and Hale, his hand at my nape, grounding me, his breath ragged, his voice reverent as he murmurs.
'Good girl.'
The words send another ripple of pleasure through me, and I gasp, my body trembling, my head dropping forward as I try to catch my breath.
And they're there.

All of them.

Holding me.

Keeping me.

'Hale...' my voice is barely a whisper, breathless, shattered, my body still trembling from the last orgasm that tore through me. 'I want you-' my breath hitches as Carter shifts beneath me, his hands holding me steady. 'I want all of you.'

Hale's sharp breath is the only answer I get at first. Then, a low, 'Quinn...'

It's not a refusal.

I push back against Laurent's chest, my head tilting up, lips parting in silent invitation. He groans softly, his fingers tightening on my jaw as his mouth captures mine. It's deep, possessive - his tongue sweeps against mine as I open for him, as I surrender to him, as I let him take what he wants, what I want to give.

And then behind me, Hale moves.

The bed shifts, the heat of his body pressing closer, his hand skating down my back, over the curve of my spine, lower, lower. My breath stutters, my fingers clutching at Carter's chest as my world shrinks to sensation.

I'm shaking, my thighs tight around Carter, my whole body caught in an unbearable, delicious tension as Hale's touch grows firmer, his fingers slick, teasing.

For a moment, I can't breathe.

For a moment, I don't know if I can take it.

And then Carter strokes my cheek, his thumb dragging across my lips, Laurent's mouth still on mine, devouring me, and Hale- *God, Hale*- his breath shudders hot against my back as he pushes forward, stretching me, filling me in a way I have never been filled before.

I choke on a gasp, my fingers clutching harder at Carter's chest as a mix of pleasure and pressure steals the air from my lungs.

'Breathe,' Carter murmurs, voice thick, deep. His hands slide up my thighs, holding me open, keeping me steady as I tremble between them. 'Relax... let him in.'

I do.

I exhale shakily, my body giving way to it, giving way to them, stretching, accommodating, taking everything they offer as Hale moves deeper.

I whimper into Laurent's mouth, my body electric, on fire, shaking with pleasure so sharp it borders on pain. But God, *it's perfect*. The overwhelming fullness, the unbearable tension, the heat of them surrounding me, inside me, taking me.

Hale groans against my shoulder, his breath ragged, his hands gripping my waist, keeping me still as he buries himself to the hilt.

I'm shaking.

I'm too full.

And yet I'm not full enough.

Laurent swipes his thumb over my lips, coaxing them apart. 'Open for me, chérie.'

And I do.

I let him guide me, my lips parting wider, my tongue flicking over the tip of him as he exhales hard through his nose. He watches me with dark, molten eyes as I take him deeper, hollowing my cheeks, giving him everything I have left to give.

And then, they move.

All of them.

A choked sound escapes my throat as Carter thrusts up, as Hale rocks into me from behind, slow at first, careful, until he realises I don't want careful.

I want *more*.

Laurent curses, his fingers twisting into my hair as I moan around him, my body melting, tightening, pulling them all deeper, taking them, wanting them, needing them like I've never needed anything in my life.

I'm everywhere at once.

Split apart.

Completely filled.

Airtight.

A desperate whimper vibrates against Laurent's length as I come apart between them, as pleasure slams through me like lightning, leaving me shaking, gasping, drowning in sensation. I hear their groans, feel the way they shudder, the way their grips tighten, the way their bodies take me harder, deeper, as if they need this just as much as I do.

And God, I love it.

I love how I'm theirs, how I've let them break me, unravel me, remake me.

Carter's hands are unrelenting on my hips as he pounds into me, his voice tight, desperate. Hale's body shakes behind me, his breath ragged, his teeth dragging over my shoulder as he gives in, gives me everything, fills me completely - fucking my tight little asshole.

Laurent swears softly as I tighten around them all, his hands trembling as he grips my jaw, his hips stuttering forward.

And then - we're falling.

All of us.

The world narrows to this, to the desperate, breathless moment where pleasure tips us over the edge and takes us all with it.

Carter gasps beneath me, a rough, guttural sound as his fingers bite into my hips, holding me down as he thrusts deep, shuddering, filling me.

Hale's grip tightens, his hands flexing against my waist, his rhythm faltering as he groans into my shoulder, his whole body stiffening behind me before he spills inside me too, hot and deep.

Laurent jerks beneath my lips, his fingers tangling in my hair as he thrusts once, twice, then collapses, his head tilting back as he comes undone against my tongue.

And I feel it all.

Every pulse. Every throb. Every drop of them spilling into me, onto me, marking me, claiming me, consuming me.

It wrecks me.

Overwhelms me.

Steals my breath, my mind, my entire self.

I shudder violently, my body locking tight between them as the sensation crashes over me, my own release hitting so hard, so deep, so utterly consuming that I can't hold back the cry that breaks from my throat.

I convulse, gasping, my entire body pulsing around them, tightening, gripping, holding them deep as my orgasm explodes like wildfire through every nerve, every cell.

Carter curses beneath me, his hands bruising against my thighs as I squeeze around him, milking him, dragging out every last tremor.

Hale groans into my neck, his hips jerking, his teeth dragging over my skin, holding back the sound that threatens to break from his chest as he gives in completely, emptying himself into me, his body wracked with tremors.

Laurent sways, his head lolling forward, his fingers shaking against my scalp as his own release coats my tongue, my lips, my chin.

It's too much.

I tremble violently, every pulse of them inside me, against me, filling me, dripping from me making me spiral deeper, higher, beyond anything I've ever known.

I gasp as the last waves of my climax steal the breath from my lungs, my vision whiting out, my limbs weak, my pulse a frantic, desperate *pound pound pound* between my ribs.

And then, silence.

My body quivers, pinned between them, weighted by their warmth, their pleasure, their release.

Hale's breath is ragged against my skin, his hands still gripping my hips as if to keep himself tethered.

Carter groans softly beneath me, shifting, his chest heaving, his hands trailing up my back in lazy circles.

Laurent sighs, his fingers stroking through my hair, down my damp cheek, his touch reverent, worshipping.

I did this.

I took them all.

I made them break.

And God, I've never felt so utterly wrecked, so complete, so perfectly ruined.

My breath stutters as my senses slowly return, every nerve still alight, every inch of me still buzzing, soaked in their pleasure, in their sweat, in their heat.

I feel them everywhere.

Inside me.

On my skin.

In my bones.

I shudder again, gasping, my lips parting - but there are no words for this, no way to explain the way my body feels, the way my *soul* feels.

Laurent hums lazily, his thumb tracing the corner of my mouth before dragging down, pressing against my swollen lower lip. 'Breathe, chérie,' he murmurs. 'You're shaking.'

I am.

I can't stop.

Carter's hands tighten on my back, grounding me, holding me against him.

Hale exhales against my shoulder, his fingers flexing once before he slowly, carefully, eases out of me, a soft groan escaping his lips.

I whimper at the loss, at the slick warmth that follows, at the way my body clenches involuntarily, desperate to keep them inside me.

Carter groans as well, his hands steadying me as I slowly lift my hips, his release slipping from me, mixing with Hale's, with Laurent's, with all of them.

I'm ruined.

Utterly, devastatingly, beautifully ruined.

And I don't regret a single second of it.

*

Warmth.

That's the first thing I feel - the delicious, unshakable heat of them - of all of them - wrapped around me, against me, inside me.

Carter's chest at my back, rising and falling in steady rhythm, his arm heavy over my waist.

Laurent's leg tangled with mine, his fingers curled lazily around my wrist, keeping me close even in sleep.

Hale's warmth against my front, solid, protective, his breath soft against my hair, his hand resting low over my hip.

The cabin sways gently, the faint hum of the engines a soothing lull beneath the weight of their bodies.

I don't want to move.

I *never* want to move.

Not from this bed, from this moment, this afterglow, this perfect, satiated bliss that still pulses through my limbs like warm, honeyed liquor.

My body hums with remnants of them, with the memory of Carter beneath me, his hands gripping tight as I rode him, with the way Hale took me so completely, filling me where no man ever had before, with the taste of Laurent against my tongue as he unraveled, giving me everything.

God, I can still feel them.

Still feel how they ruined me. How they owned me. How I let them.

I shift just slightly, thighs pressing together, heat blooming all over again, the evidence of our sins still damp, still slick between my legs.

And I can't stop the small, breathy whimper that escapes my lips.

Then-

A crackle of static.

A voice over the intercom.

'Cabin crew, prepare for landing.'

My eyes pop open.

Shit.

A rush of awareness slams into me, dragging me from the haze of pleasure straight into reality.

We're landing.

Landing.

In Dubai.

And I am very, *very* naked, tangled in three very naked men, dripping in evidence of all the filthy, forbidden things we did together.

Holy. Fucking. Shit.

I suck in a breath, my pulse leaping, my mind spinning.

Carter shifts behind me, grumbling something incoherent as his grip tightens on my waist. Laurent sighs deeply, nuzzling closer. Hale exhales against my hair, his hold possessive even in sleep.

I'm surrounded.

Pinned.

And in less than twenty minutes, this jet is going to touch down, and I have to walk out there like I didn't just let these three men fuck me senseless at 40,000 feet.

Shit, shit, shit.

I start to move, wiggling free, slipping from beneath Carter's arm, from Laurent's grip, from Hale's warmth.

They grumble sleepily in protest, but I move quickly, grabbing at sheets, covering myself, scrambling for the edge of the bed.

I need to get up, clean up, find my uniform-

If I even have a uniform left.

A low chuckle rumbles behind me. 'Going somewhere, chérie?'

Laurent.

Of course.

I glance back, finding all three of them watching me now, sleepy-eyed, smug, utterly, sinfully satisfied.

And I know that this look, this feeling, this moment - it's not over.

Not by a long shot.

I scramble from the bed, yanking the sheets around me as I stagger, my legs still shaky, sore, used. Ruined in the most *delicious* way.

The plane dips slightly, the descent beginning, and I curse under my breath as I glance around, eyes scanning the room in search of-

My uniform.

Or what's left of it.

I spot my blouse crumpled in a heap near the foot of the bed, my skirt flung over the arm of the leather chair, my lace panties discarded, glistening on the carpet.

Shit.

I bend quickly, grabbing at my clothes, but before I can make a run for the bathroom to fix myself, a firm hand catches my wrist.

'Now, now, cherie. No need to be shy,' Laurent purrs, his grip lazy but strong as he tugs me back toward the bed, my sheet slipping just enough to expose my bare shoulder.

Carter hums from his spot still lounging against the pillows. 'What's the rush? Pretty sure they won't let us off the plane until we taxi to the gate. Plenty of time to... *debrief*.'

I glare at them.

'*Debrief?*' I snatch my blouse from the floor. 'You mean watch me run around trying to look remotely professional while you all sit there being smug?'

Hale smirks. 'I mean... it's a good view.'

Carter snickers. Laurent just shrugs, his eyes trailing down the length of my body, completely unashamed.

I throw my blouse at his face.

He catches it effortlessly, chuckling. 'You wound me, chérie.'

'You deserve it,' I grumble, shimmying into my skirt, but my legs are so weak, so unsteady that I nearly topple over.

Hale reaches out, steadying me with a firm hand on my hip, and my whole body clenches, memories of the last few hours flashing like hot film reels in my mind.

His voice is low, gravelly. 'You okay?'

I swallow hard, nodding. But my pulse is still racing, my skin still flushed, and the fact that I have all three of them watching me - watching my every movement, my every struggle, my every stuttering breath - makes my entire body feel like it's still on fire.

I grab my blouse from Laurent's lap, buttoning it as quickly as my trembling fingers will allow.

'Quinn.'

I glance up at Carter.

He smirks. 'You might wanna-' he gestures vaguely.

I frown. 'What?'

Laurent leans in, voice rich with amusement. 'Your buttons, chérie. Wrong holes.'

I look down.

'Shit.'

I've completely mismatched them. One side of my blouse is higher than the other, and my bra is still mostly visible.

Carter outright laughs, shaking his head as he stands from the bed, reaching for his pants.

'She's flustered,' Laurent teases.

'I am *not* flustered,' I snap, my fingers fumbling as I redo each button properly.

Hale just smirks knowingly as he fastens his belt, watching me struggle with unhurried ease.

'You look cute like this,' Carter muses, zipping himself up, his tone full of mischief. 'All out of sorts. All messed up. All-' his eyes darken. '-ruined.'

Heat rushes straight between my legs.

'I hate you,' I mutter.

'Liar.'

I don't argue.

Instead, I shove my feet into my heels, wobbling slightly as I regain my balance, yanking my hair into some semblance of order, my cheeks burning as all three of them simply smirk at me.

The intercom crackles again.

'Final approach into Dubai International Airport. Cabin crew, take your seats.'

'*Shit.*'

I glance at them one last time, at the wicked, satisfied glints in their eyes, the way they're already planning their next move, their next game, their next way to ruin me all over again.

And as I straighten my blouse, smooth my skirt, lift my chin high, I realise something.

This might be the end of the flight.

But it's just the beginning of whatever this is.

Whatever we are.

And for the first time in my life, I don't care about the

destination.
 Because the journey is just too damn fun.

*

EPILOGUE

The plane is still, the engines silenced, the gentle sway of flight now a memory. Through the open door, the golden glow of Dubai spills inside, warm and inviting, a stark contrast to the cool, composed veneer I'm desperately trying to maintain.

I stand at the exit, posture straight, uniform pristine, hands clasped before me as Callum and Reynolds flank my sides.

Professional.

Presentable.

Poised.

And utterly ruined.

Behind me, in the cabin, Carter, Hale, and Laurent gather their things. Slow. Leisurely. Taking their damn time. Stretching. Buttoning. Running hands through mussed-up hair.

I did that to them.

I refuse to look.

Refuse to acknowledge the heated hum still coursing through my veins, the ghostly imprint of their hands, their mouths, their bodies.

Instead, I focus on the glinting floor, on the faint reflections of overhead lights. On not combusting.

Callum leans in, voice low. 'You're walking a little funny.'

I ignore him.

Reynolds huffs a quiet laugh beside me.

I grit my teeth, fixing my gaze straight ahead.

Callum continues, relentless. 'Did you-' he pauses, just for effect, the bastard '-get much sleep?'

I inhale sharply, barely restraining my very non-professional response.

'Hmm ' he taps his fingers against his belt, as though thinking. 'Or did something... keep you up?'

I blink. Breathe.

Do not react.

Do not let them win.

But I hear them behind me. The deep, familiar timbre of Carter's chuckle. The husky lilt of Laurent's murmured French. The unmistakable sound of Hale exhaling, like he's shaking his head at both of them.

Like he knows exactly what Callum is doing.

Like they all do.

And I swear I can still feel their eyes on me.

Still feel them everywhere.

I steady myself, spine straight, chin high.

And I say nothing.

Because I refuse to give anyone the satisfaction.

Even if my thighs are trembling. Even if my skin is flushed. Even if the moment Carter reaches my side, standing before me, eyes dark and knowing and hungry, I forget how to breathe entirely.

Hale moves first.

No hesitation, no backward glance - just quiet, measured strides as he steps forward, reaching for each pilot's hand in turn. A firm shake. A murmured thanks. The picture of composure.

And then he turns to me.

I force myself to meet his gaze, not to drop my chin, not to let my breath hitch as his dark eyes sweep over me, slow and deliberate, his expression unreadable.

But my composure? It's trembling.

Because I still feel him. Still feel the way he pressed me into the galley door, the way his breath stuttered against my skin, the way he filled me so completely, so utterly, until I forgot where I ended and he began.

And now?

Now, there's nothing but space between us. Space, and searing, unbearable memory.

His mouth presses into the faintest smirk - like he knows.

Then, finally, he nods.

Simple.

Brief.

Devastating.

Then he's gone.

Stepping past me, down the short ramp and into the golden glow of Dubai.

And I let him go.

Even if every muscle in my body wants to reach out.

Even if every nerve is still attuned to him.

Even if my hands twitch at my sides.

Because he's gone now.

And Laurent is next.

Laurent takes his time.

Where Hale was quiet, restrained, Laurent is anything but. He strolls forward like he owns the damn cabin, slinging his expensive duffel over one shoulder as he stops before Callum and Reynolds, offering them each a lazy, knowing handshake.

Then, he turns to me.

And the look in his eyes? Absolutely sinful.

His smirk is sharp, wicked. The kind of expression that threatens to unravel every last thread of my carefully stitched composure.

'Chérie,' he purrs, his voice pitched just low enough for me alone. 'You'll miss me, won't you?'

I swallow hard. Keep my hands clasped at my front, white-knuckled. Steady. 'You're a hard man to forget, Mr Laurent.'

His grin widens. 'Ah. But forgetting is not the same as missing, non?'

I inhale sharply, and he watches - actually watches - the way my chest rises and falls, eyes gleaming like he's still savoring the memory of me beneath him.

And then - the bastard leans in.

Not touching, not quite, but so close that I catch the scent of him, dark and spiced, mingled with champagne and the faintest trace of me still lingering on his skin.

'Perhaps,' he murmurs, 'I should give you something else to remember me by. A little souvenir, hmm?'

Heat flares in my cheeks, racing down my spine. Callum shifts beside me, watching.

Laurent chuckles under his breath, dropping his voice even lower. 'Ah, but you already have one, don't you? Deep inside. A little something to tide you over until next time.'

Oh. My. God.

My knees actually threaten to give out.

Laurent must sense it, because his smirk deepens, his lips parting as though he's about to say something even more scandalous-

'Laurent,' Carter drawls behind him, amusement laced through his voice. 'If you torment her any further, she might actually combust.'

Laurent sighs dramatically, stepping back just enough to let me breathe again, though his eyes promise everything.

'Fine, fine,' he presses a hand over his heart, mock wounded. 'I'll leave our sweet Quinn in peace... for now.'

Then, with one last unapologetic glance over my body, he winks - actually winks - and saunters off into the Dubai night.

Leaving me weak, shaken, and aching.

And then there's only one left.

Carter.

Carter doesn't rush. He moves like a man who knows exactly what he does to me.

Like a man who knows I still feel him inside me.

He shakes Callum's hand first, then Reynolds', his charm as effortless as ever, a polite nod, a smooth goodbye. But when he turns to me - really turns to me - the air thickens.

I stand my ground, but it's impossible to look unaffected. Not when every part of me is trembling, my skin still flushed, my breath not quite steady.

His gaze drags over me, slow, drinking me in from my hair - still neatly pinned, but he knows what it looked like tangled in his hands - down to my uniform, tidied, composed, put back together. But not untouched. Not untouched at all.

His smirk is lazy, knowing.

God, I hate him.

God, I want him.

'Goodbye, Quinn,' his voice is low, smooth as silk, but there's something else underneath. Something just for me.

I open my mouth, but no words come out.

And then, he touches me.

Just his fingers, just a brush against the inside of my wrist - barely anything. And yet, it feels like a live wire against my skin, my pulse leaping, my knees weakening.

He feels it.

His smirk deepens, devastating, and then he turns -

walking away, just like that.

But then-

He stops.

Right at the threshold, just feet from Hale.

And he turns back.

My breath catches as he studies me, eyes dark, lips curling into something that undoes me.

He knows.

Laurent knows, standing just outside, arms folded, a knowing smirk on his lips. Hale, too, watching me, watching Carter, watching everything.

And Carter doesn't lower his voice when he speaks.

He wants them to hear.

'Come to dinner tonight.'

Not a question.

Not a suggestion.

A command.

'Eight o'clock,' his head tilts slightly. 'The penthouse suite.'

My lips part, my pulse pounding, my lungs barely working.

Hale shifts slightly beside him, silent, unreadable, but I see it - the way his shoulders rise, the way his hands curl into fists, like he's waiting.

Laurent lets out a low chuckle, muttering something under his breath that I can't quite hear.

Carter just watches me.

Waits.

I don't answer.

I can't.

Because every part of me is screaming.

And he knows it.

His smirk lingers for a fraction longer - one last victory. Then, without another word, he turns and steps off the plane, disappearing into the terminal with the others.

And I exhale.

A sharp, shuddering breath.

My fingers are trembling. My pulse is roaring. My body aching.

Because this isn't over.

This is just the beginning.

And I am *so* fucking ready.

THE END

Want more? Snuggle in for a snowbound threesome with Kinky Kayleigh, Woodsman Sam and Bestie Becca in **One More Swing: A First Time FFM Christmas Menage**

Keep reading for a sample chapter.

SAMPLE CHAPTER - ONE MORE SWING

There was no other way. She simply had no other choice.

Kayleigh had spent several minutes weighing up all the alternatives open to her, but after careful consideration, she had come to the conclusion that her solution was in fact, the only way forward.

The last resort.

'Sam?' she said as she stood tangled in the mass of fairy lights that had defeated her. 'Get the axe.'

A mop of messy dark bed hair attached to a grizzled bearded face appeared in the doorway to their kitchen with a frown on. 'The axe? What for?' he asked.

'*This*,' she said, holding up a wild bundle of the offending illuminations.

The mop of hair began to laugh. 'No,' he said, disappearing.

'Sam,' she shouted, her lips curling into a grin. '*Axe.*'

'You're not using the axe,' he called, his voice so laden that she could practically feel him shaking his head as he spoke.

'I *am*,' she said, posing defiantly as she raised her voice. 'I'm *done*. There's no other way. This has to end, here and *now*.'

Sam reappeared, his eyes wide and his mouth taunting her with mirth. 'Alright, calm down Bateman.'

'Don't tell me to calm down,' she snapped. 'Or I'll wrap you up in this too.'

'Give it here. Let me have a go,' he said, sauntering over with all the confident swagger of a cowboy in a brothel.

'Be my guest,' she said, throwing him the coil, which fell short by several feet as it caught around her foot.

She shook it free with an excitable grin, her whole body buzzing with excitement because, despite her defeat at the gnarled and twisted coil of the reclaimed fairy lights that had so completely thwarted her attempts to rescue them, nothing was going to darken her day, because today... Becca was coming.

Becca.

Becca was Kayleigh's best and closest friend. She was also Kayleigh's first, longest and *hardest* forbidden girl crush, and this meant a lot to someone who had spent most of her life extremely confused about her sexuality.

Becca was also the reason that Kayleigh was putting so much effort into decorating because her best friend *loved* Christmas, and right now her best friend was hurting, and Christmas was going to solve that.

She was sure of it.

For several minutes Sam stood as Kayleigh watched, her arms folded with a satisfied grin as her fiancé tried and failed over and over again to fathom the ouroboros loop of glimmering lights that had defeated her before, at last, he took a deep breath, lowered his gaze and nodded glumly.

'Fetch the axe.'

Kayleigh bounced up and down on the spot with glee before bounding out of the toasty room, the wood fire burning bright in the corner.

Quickly she sailed through their little kitchen, taking a moment to inhale the scent of chilli bubbling on the hob - *Becca's favourite* - before pulling open the door to the workroom with a little too much gusto.

Unhooking their largest wood axe from its place on the wall she let out an entirely child-like squeal as she gripped it in both hands, before bounding back through and sliding into her thick winter boots without pause.

Sam, clearly on the same wavelength as her now, had already proceeded out back, donning his down-filled body warmer and carrying the wild nest of wires and broken bulbs unceremoniously above his head before dumping it on the wide trunk that had endured so much already this winter.

Kayleigh, too excited to wrap herself up, shivered in the bitter cold as she trudged through the snow toward him, proffering the axe with both hands and giggling as he accepted it with a pretend heft, as though it weighed several times more than its actual mass. Then she settled back and watched with glee as he raised the handle high above his head and held it there, pausing for a moment for dramatic effect.

'I feel like you should do this,' he said, with a sideways glance.

'Uh-uh,' she said, stepping back further as her tummy twisted and her thighs fluttered. 'There's nothing hotter than watching you cut wood.'

Sam frowned. 'Cutting fairy lights does it for you too?'

'*Yes*,' whispered Kayleigh. 'Shut up and cut.'

Thud.

Down came the blade in a sharp flash, slicing clean through the bundle of wires, a couple of the tiny bulbs exploding with a tinkle as the sensation thrummed through her.

Fuck yes.

Kayleigh bit down on her lower lip, her tummy twisting as Sam tugged the bit free, the toe of the blade catching in the trunk as he hefted it, the sound of splintering wood echoing through their little patch of woodland and sending a few brave birds fluttering and her heart racing.

'Now do a log,' she whispered as she tried to control herself, her warm breath billowing out into the cool midday air.

'You're going to freeze to death,' Sam laughed as he grabbed a particularly chunky one from the nearby pile and placed it in position, lining it up and standing back.

'Trust me,' she said, her eyes tracing the definition of his body through the thick warmer and ribbed white wool jumper he wore over his ripped chest. 'I won't.'

Thud.

The moment the axe came down, splitting the log into two even halves, something *pinged* inside of her. This was her favourite part of each day out here on the edge of their little forest, tucked away, off-grid and all warm and snugly in the log cabin that they called home.

Sam cutting wood.

The act did something primal to her, something that she felt deeply ashamed of on one level - *the same one that decried the patriarchy and embraced love in all its forms* - and that she indulged wholeheartedly on another.

Bottom line? Watching her fiancé chop wood was her *kink*, and she was already feeling stupidly horny. It wasn't helping that the idea of Becca staying with them over Christmas had fired up her imagination in all *manner* of naughty ways.

'*Yes*,' she whispered, suddenly feeling overcome as she

quivered, several naughty images striking her mind's eye all at once as she wavered. 'Take me inside and *fuck* me.'

Please.

Sam dropped the axe so fast the bit sliced clean through the snow and stuck fast in the frozen mud beneath, the handle quivering for a heartbeat as the sensation reverberated through her chest.

Then her fiancé grinned, pounced, and picked her up bodily, throwing her tiny frame over his shoulder as she squealed, and marched her toward the open door, the orange glow of warmth and flickering flames burning bright within.

Sam wasted no time as he kicked the back door shut, thrusting Kayleigh down on the thick wooden table he'd hewn from an old oak tree six months before and then kissing her hard as he parted her thighs and pulled her roughly toward him.

Kayleigh moaned softly, embracing his raw strength and passion as she felt his thick member press against her warmth through his tight jeans, and she couldn't help herself as she twisted her hips and rubbed hard against him.

Sam *did things* to her, he triggered things inside of her that she had never fully understood. Kayleigh had never fully identified as straight, and yet the first moment she'd met Sam, *all* bets had been off.

He *growled* as she teased him, pulling back and freezing as she bit down on his lip, keeping him in place as she looked up into his wild eyes, the world holding its breath… and then ever so gently she let go as his hand rose slowly up her side, over the curve of her breast, across her shoulder, then up to her neck until finally, he cupped her cheek as they looked at one another, his eyes like black holes, her whole being forever within his event horizon, tumbling and stretching.

And then it was back on.

Kayleigh tore at Sam's gilet, deftly unzipping it with one

hand as her other worked his belt, wasting no time as she unbuckled him but forgetting for a moment to unbutton him as she jammed her hand into his pants, pulling a hasty retreat as she laughed before trying again and bristling with excitement as her fingers closed around his thickness.

Up and down she pumped, curling her small hand around his girth as he kissed her, his fingers tugging at her skin-tight jeans and pulling her panties away with them as he tugged them down past her ankles, tearing off both boots and one sock as an afterthought and sending them sailing as one before turning back and admiring her like a hunter, just before the kill.

She tingled as he looked at her sat before him on their shining table, basking in the golden light of the fire, her fierce eyes like flames, her fleece jumper still wrapped around her, her gilet hanging loose, her naked thighs parted, her pussy bare and glistening.

She widened herself as his gaze lowered, letting him look, letting him drink her in, and then she took one finger and licked it and ran it down over her tummy, across her mound and down between her lips where she slowly circled herself as her fiancé grinned.

'Fuck,' he whispered, shaking his head, his hands loosening his buttons and then dropping his pants altogether, before unzipping his body warmer and tearing off all his remaining layers.

Kayleigh's breathing fastened as he stood before her, his powerful abs glistening in the flickering flames, his mesmerising eyes dark and full of lust, his cock throbbing and proud. Then he moved forward again and she gasped and moaned in anticipation of his touch.

The moment his lips met hers his cock sank into her, her pussy already so wet that he met no resistance, the entirety of his thick powerful member sliding in all the way to the hilt, filling her *entirely* in a heartbeat as he kissed her, and making her whole again as her body trembled with pleasure.

'Oh *yes*,' she cried, nuzzling into his neck as the sensation overwhelmed her, her eyes closing as he pulled back, her body tensing *befor-*

He thrust again and the world spun as a wall of ecstasy crashed through her like a rogue wave on a wild ocean, rocking her body and making her buck and quiver.

'*Yes, oh fuck*,' she gasped, her eyes rolling back. '*Ye-*'

Again he thrust, powering into her harder and harder with every passing second as though he was an *animal*, barely in control of himself, his lust for her sending him wild, and yet he was in complete control and she felt it.

'*Fuck*,' he whispered. 'You're so goddamned tight, Kayleigh. I fucking *love* your little pussy.'

'Yes,' she whispered. 'It's yours, *fuck* my pussy.'

Sam growled as he hardened inside of her, thrusting even harder in response to her words, his fingers digging into her ass as he pulled her forward. At the same time, she tugged hard at her top, pulling her woollen jumper up and over her head and sending it sailing as Sam's hands pulled down her bra cup and wrapped his lips around her nipple.

'Oh, Sam,' she cried, burying her face in his hair. '*Yes. Yes.*'

And then there it was, like a freight train in a dark tunnel, barrelling toward her so fast she wouldn't have had time to move if she'd wanted to.

Yes.

'*Fuck*,' she cried as she came, hard and fast and dirty, her pussy contracting and *squeezing* her man's cock so tight that he shuddered and twitched and moaned and *burst*.

'*Yes*,' he groaned in surprise as his seed flowed, his entire girth thrumming and throbbing, undulating within her tight little walls as rope after rope of his warmth flowed into her.

'Oh, *Sam*,' she whispered as their eyes met, the warmth of

the fire suddenly overwhelming as her senses returned, her naked body - all exposed except for one knee-high sock - covered in a sheen of glistening happiness as her fiancé's eyes glowed with wonder.

'Fuck, I love you,' he whispered, kissing her lips and thrusting softly, his cock still mostly hard as he softened inside her.

'I love you too,' she said. 'Don't move. I like feeling you inside of me.'

Sam grinned, licking his lips as he rocked back and forth gently, holding her tight still as he stroked the bare skin of her hips with his thumbs.

'You are incredible,' he said, shaking, as he licked his lips and breathed.

Sam always became mushy after they made love, and Kayleigh loved it. His outdoor, rugged persona had another side, and only she got to see it, and only in the afterglow of their most intimate moments, where he'd profess his adulation for her over and over as they held one another. In those moments she felt like a princess, as though she was the most special girl in the world, and it filled her with boundless joy.

'You're not too bad yourself,' she grinned, her eyes tearing up as she took a long deep breath. 'For a boy.'

'I mean it,' he said. 'You are everything to me.'

She blushed, looking down as she ran her fingers over his sticky abs, his cock still twitching inside of her, leaking slowly between her lips before slipping gently out and leaving her bereft.

He stepped back, breathing out and closing his eyes before reaching for her hand and pulling her up to sitting, his eyes tracing her curves as she perched upright.

Kayleigh grinned as she felt his seed dripping gently into a sticky pool between her thighs and as she closed her legs and leaned forward with her elbows on her knees, she nodded toward the fireplace.

'Might need to throw another log or two on there, before it gets cold,' she grinned. 'Just a little *chop-chop*.'

Sam laughed, throwing his head back and shaking his mop of hair as he tugged his jeans almost back into place, his cock at half mast and still glistening, framed in the unclosed gap.

'You're insatiable,' he said, grinning.

'And you love it,' she whispered, setting her feet down on the floor and lowering herself down before turning around and bending over the table. 'You wanna come in my ass too?'

She looked back to find Sam's dark eyes wandering down over her spine and tracing the curve of her bare cheeks before licking his lips, and dropping his jeans again.

That was one of the wonders of Sam - he was *always* ready.

Taking hold of his instantly hard cock he took one smooth step forward and lined himself up as she braced, his free hand warm as he ran his fingers up and over her soaking wet lips and then circled her asshole, and then before she could even close her eyes she felt him press the tip of his cock against her tightest opening *an-*

'*Oh fuck*,' she cried.

He was in.

'Oh *yes*,' he moaned with delight as he pushed his way deeper and deeper into her, her tight little hole stretching over his thick glans, squeezing into her and making her jaw drop open, and then every inch of his member slid slowly inside of her as she gasped and held her breath until he was *all* the way in, and *thrumming*.

'Fuck,' she gasped. 'You're so big.'

'*Ah shit*,' moaned Sam, already twitching and pulsing as he gently pulled back. 'I'm going to come really fast.'

'Yes, baby,' she whispered, nodding. 'Come in my ass.'

'*Oh fuck*,' he groaned, his head back and his body

quivering in pure delight as she tingled with taboo, his hands gripping her hips tight as he thrust once, *twic-*

'*Aaah,*' he moaned as he fell forward and into her, his cock throbbing *hard* inside of her as he came again, his body twitching as he pressed into her, emptying himself completely as he moaned so hard and for so long that he ran out of breath.

Kayleigh melted beneath him as he held her tight, his limp arms like lead as he fought for consciousness, slowly coming back to life and holding her warmly, his muscular frame enveloping her tiny one, his cock still twitching inside her ass as he cocooned her, his head beside hers, his warm cheek bristly, his fingers interlocking with hers.

Heaven.

'Fuck,' he whispered. 'I love y-'

Silence.

'I love you too,' she whispered, smiling.

She liked breaking her man and turning him into a quivering mess where he couldn't even form or find sentences, just muttering vague utterances and murmurings of contentment and pure satisfaction.

It was amazing, and she *lived* for it. If love was a drug, then she was high as fuck on it, and it felt *incredible,* and to top it off, in just over an hour, Becca would be here too.

Becca.

The *other* love of her life.

*

Want more? Snuggle in for a Christmas threesome with Kinky Kayleigh, Woodsman Sam and Bestie Becca in **One More Swing: A First Time FFM Christmas Menage**

THANK YOU

Thank you for reading **Three Passenger's for Quinn**

You can now **rate my books without leaving a review on Amazon**, but if you do have a few moments to spare, I'd love to hear your thoughts.

Even just a couple of lines makes a **HUGE** difference, and I would be so grateful. It really helps other amazing readers like yourself feel *confident* in giving a **new author a try.**

Subscribe to my newsletter to get your FREE COPY of Play Swing.
Stay subscribed for all my latest news, new releases, deals, and more free stories!

Follow me on Amazon, Twitter, Instagram, Goodreads & BookBub

Three Passengers for Quinn

Stories by Brianna Skylark

Erotic Swingers

Be With Us - An Urban Foursome Love Story

Play With Us - An Urban Foursome Game Night Fantasy

Come With Us - An Urban Foursome Vacation Romance

Stay With Us - An Urban Foursome Swingers Ménage

The Paramour - An Erotic Victorian Ménage

Fantasy Swingers

Tushie - A Taboo Tale of Forbidden Love

Muffin - A First Time FFM Ménage Romance

Bootie - A Hotwife Fantasy MFM Ménage

Cupcake - A Wife Swap Swingers Tale

Peach - A Penthouse Swingers Party

Petal - A Swingers Vacation Fantasy

Pumpkin - A Swingers Murder Mystery

Precious - A Swingers Wedding Fantasy

Snowdrop - A Secret Santa Wife Swap

FFM Threesome and Ménage Romance

The More the Merrier: A First Time FFM Christmas Threesome

His Birthday Treat: A First Time FFM Birthday Threesome

Their Best Friend: An FFM Mountain Threesome

Her Maid of Honor: An FFM Bridesmaid Threesome

Santa's Naughty Elves: An FFM Christmas Threesome

Their Perfect Nanny: A Steamy FFM Threesome Romance

Shared in Paris: A Steamy FFM Threesome Romance

Three's Company: An FFM Striptease Board Game Threesome

Sharing Their Secret: A Passionate FFM Threesome Romance

Tangled in Paradise: A Tropical FFM Threesome Romance

Silver Fox Romance - Jack & Anna

Sinful and Sweet - A Silver Fox Age Gap Romance

Angel of Sin - A Silver Fox Age Gap Romance

Dripping with Sin - A Silver Fox Age Gap Romance

Mortal Sin - A Silver Fox Age Gap Romance

Eternal Sin - A Silver Fox Age Gap Romance

Reverse Harem Romance

Three Wishes for Cassie: An Airtight Reverse Harem Ménage

Three Gifts for Holly: A Christmas Reverse Harem Ménage

Three Bids for Lottie: A Strip Poker Reverse Harem Auction

Three Lessons for Maisie: A Ski Resort Reverse Harem Ménage

Three Passengers for Quinn: An Airborne Reverse Harem Ménage

Forbidden Nanny - A Single Dad Age Gap Romance

Billionaires Swingers Romance

Sweet and Discreet - Maid for the Billionaire

Sparkle and Spice - Falling for the Billionaire

Squeaky and Clean - Romancing the Billionaire

Naughty and Nice - Sharing the Billionaire

Stars and Shine - A Wedding for the Billionaire

First Time Swingers

Into the Swing - A First Time Wife Swap Fantasy

Back Swing - A Truth or Dare Swingers Fantasy

Hot Swing - A Hot Tub Swingers Fantasy

Mistletoe Swing - A Christmas Wife Swap Fantasy

Little Swing - An MFM Lockdown Ménage

Power Swing - A Billionaire Swingers Fantasy

Cyber Swing - A Swipe Right Wife Swap Fantasy

Jingle Swing - A Christmas Foursome Fantasy

Strip Swing - A Best Friends Striptease Foursome

Dark Swing - A Desert Riders Wife Swap Fantasy

Highland Swing - A Best Friends Birthday Wife Swap

One More Swing - An First Time FFM Christmas Ménage

Forbidden Temptations

Throwback - An Enemies to Lovers Fantasy

Fifth Base - A Cheeky First Time Fantasy

Sharing Rose - A Romantic MFM Mountain Ménage

Read the Amazon Top 50 Bestselling Erotic Swingers Series

Five deliciously naughty novels filled with saucy swinger fun, and filthy forbidden romance.

Blissfully married bombshell Emilia has never been with anyone but her rugged high-school sweetheart Cass. He's confident, strong, dark and handsome, and he's all hers... but innocent Emilia has a burning desire.

She wants to be touched and kissed, and held... and shared, in every imaginable way.

Indulge in the carnal temptations of Emilia, Cassian, Amy and Mark as they embark on a wild, romantic and deeply erotic adventure into the world of swinging, decadence and unconventional love.

*'This is **so hot** that **several timeouts** were absolutely necessary!'*

*'A really **fantastic read**, everyone enjoying themselves, **no humiliation or angst** just good clean (or not, as the case may be) fun!'*

* * *

'Blew me away with the brilliance of the writing!'

Read the ***number one bestselling series*** on Kindle & Kindle Unlimited, and follow Emilia, Cassian, Amy and Mark as they explore their blossoming, and very *naughty* friendship across **several** lip-bitingly passionate books.

Read the #1 Bestselling Fantasy Swingers series

Innocent wife Elsie can't get enough of her **rugged and insatiable** husband Cole. But there are some things that are **off-limits, filthy...** *taboo.*

So when Cole accidentally touches her in her **most private and untouched place**, it shakes the very foundations of their marriage, leaving her desperate for more. Her newfound kink has Elsie questioning everything, including her shameful crush on her best friend Alice.

Now that **nothing is off the table** and their darkest fantasies are out in the open, can their blissful marriage survive? Or will **temptation and desire** tear them apart for good?

*'This was my **first**, and **definitely not last** read of Brianna Skylark... what are you trying to **DO** to me?!'*

*'This story is a **real breath of fresh air**. This is **super** sexy erotica. Careful where you read this one, folks!'*

*'Sensual, **stimulating**, seductive, beautiful and written with love.*

You can feel every push, every stretch!

Read the *number one bestselling series* on Kindle & Kindle Unlimited

Read the #1 Bestselling Billionaire Swingers Romance series

A mysterious billionaire, a shy hipster chick and a rebellious playboy hacker.

Sophie is broke, single and jobless. She's two weeks away from eviction and is facing the very real possibility of having to move back in with her country bumpkin parents. Then her best friend makes a throwaway comment that changes her life forever…

One day later and she's setup her own cleaning business, Sweet and Discreet. It's a one girl cleaning service with a naked twist.

Three clients, three very different encounters. All of them want her and with each sparkling visit, the tension escalates, surely it's only a matter of time before squeaky-clean Sophie gets down on her hands and knees… for some dirty fun.

*'WOW! This builds from teasing to sensual, to downright **scorching.'***

Read the *number one bestselling series* on Kindle & Kindle

Unlimited and follow Sophie as her high-end client list quickly grows. With each new skin-tingling encounter becoming naughtier than the last, will she maintain her composure and remain professional… or will she succumb to temptation, curiosity and **raw naked attraction?**

ABOUT THE AUTHOR

BRIANNA SKYLARK is the pen name of a happily married, utterly insatiable, thirty-something mother of two living in a repressed little village on the south coast of England.

She's the wife of a rugged archeologist and often likes to think she's married to Indiana Jones. Over the years she's experimented with various occupations including filmmaking, video game voiceover artist and climbing instructor, but her favourite job is her most recent one... steamy romance novelist.

She loves bringing sweet, strong, faithful and loving women to life through her books, and then introducing them to strong, kind and endearing alpha males (or sensual females) who satisfy their every desire in the bedroom and beyond.

When she's not writing, she's often found hiking or climbing in the far reaches of Scotland and Wales or exploring the woods and beaches near her home with the man of her dreams, and their two gorgeous children.

Follow me on Amazon, Twitter, Instagram, Goodreads & BookBub

Subscribe to my newsletter!

www.briannaskylark.com
Short, secret, sexy and sweet.

Printed in Dunstable, United Kingdom

78862645R00107